THE LAZARUS TREE

STEPHEN D. GRAHAM

The Lazarus Tree
© 2019 Stephen D. Graham
All rights reserved.

The Lazarus Tree is historical fiction loosely based on true events.

Editorial Assistance: Celia Springfield Graham
Cover photo (Tree): 123rf.com/ Volodymyr Goinyk
Cover Design: Hyliian Graphics
Interior design: The Author's Mentor, Ellen Sallas
www.theauthorsmentor.com

ISBN: 9781706681373
Also Available in eBook

PUBLISHED IN THE UNITED STATES OF AMERICA

Dedication

Not only did Celia stick with me on *The Lazarus Tree*, she stuck with this project thirty-plus years. For Celia's input, expertise and dedication to this project through the best and worst of times, I will always be grateful.

The Lazarus Tree

*Jesus said unto her, "I am the resurrection and the life; he that
believeth in me, though he were dead, yet shall he live. And
whosoever liveth and believeth in me shall never die..."*
(John 11:25).

The fingers of the raging fire groped across the rooftops of the
shanty houses bordering the railroad track in the moonless night sky.
The sounds of painful wailing rose into the glittering darkness as
people ran back and forth, calling out to their loved ones, hoping
they had escaped the flames. The smell of burning wood filled the
night air. At dawn, nothing remained except for one solitary chimney.
All was lost for the those who lived in this place along the railroad
tracks nearby the river.

1

IT WAS A SERIES OF ACCIDENTS THAT LED ME TO THE Lazarus Tree, or at best, a trail of chance occurrences. Tommy Morrow brought me the cameo brooch that marked the beginning of my quest. That in itself was pure chance. The fact that he found it and then brought it to me, were all random steppingstones along a lengthy and twisting path of discovery. From the first time I held the brooch in my hand, I knew there was a story to go with it. I could feel it as I tried to scrape away the tarnish time had left on the lady's face that was carved into the stone. It was almost like a crystal ball that drew me in and then held my attention. It was almost as if it called out to me begging me to find its owner and return it to them.

Tommy Morrow and my oldest son Bobby were best friends in high school. Even though they had taken different directions when they graduated, they remained close. Bobby went to college and Tommy remained here in town. He joined his father's construction business to pursue his father's dream of having a son take over where he would one day leave off. I was never entirely sure if this was Tommy's or his father's dream. Nonetheless, they were both following it. Tommy still came around, just as he had most of his life. Of course, before, he had come around to see Bobby. Now Tommy came around to get the latest news on Bobby's academic endeavors and I believe, just to talk. I always had the feeling that Tommy found it easier to talk to me than to his own father, although this was never actually discussed.

Tommy came around one Friday afternoon in March 1988. We sat out on the front porch talking about Bobby coming home for the summer and Tommy's and his father's latest construction project. I had lived here most of my life and Tommy had lived here all of his. I think everybody wondered about that one plot of ground, twenty acres or so, that ran along the railroad tracks in the center of town. That's where Tommy and his father's latest project would begin. You see, a lot of growing and changing had taken place here in my forty-five years. A lot of expansion had taken place in Bobby and Tommy's eighteen years. Oakman had grown in every direction except north; the river prevented that. However, the city grew in every other aspect, including houses, stores, and shopping centers and had probably grown five-fold in my lifetime. The progress was sometimes slow, but the growth was never-ending. Yet, as the town grew and thrived, it seems to have almost deliberately moved away from that one plot of ground along the railroad tracks.

I didn't even know that tract of land was owned by the city until Tommy told me. I always imagined it was tied up in some lengthy legal battle, a family fighting over the estate, or an owner who had long ago forgotten it was his or hers to sell. Knowing the city owned it all these years made its empty existence even more interesting. One had to wonder why when the city came into possession of such a prime piece of property in the middle of town, the city fathers went out of their way to build the last forty years elsewhere.

Granted, the railroad noise may have deterred construction in years past, but no train had gone down these tracks in three decades! Today, the tracks still ran along the twenty acres, but the end closest to the river had long ago been moved. The other end had been routed away from town and was no longer in sight, let alone close enough to be disturbing. Even Penn Road didn't really go anyplace anymore. Its boundary ran the length of this twenty acres but there were so many other routes that now there was no reason to use Penn Road. Finally, for whatever reason, the city had decided to use the land and Tommy's father, Jack Morrow, had been awarded the contract for its first building, which, Tommy had informed me, was a new library.

Tommy explained in detail how he had come across the pin; maybe a little too much detail, but I didn't interrupt. He and his father had gone alone to the site that day. Surveyors had just begun to step off and sight the boundaries of the property to ensure that the city didn't overstep its ownership. Tommy and his father had gone with a backhoe and truck to clean up the only remains of any kind of structure that existed on the site. Far in the distance beyond Penn Road perhaps three or four hundred yards, stood an old stone chimney. It sat facing the road, reaching twenty-five feet in the air. The chimney stood alone as time and progress moved all around it. The chimney stood as a reminder that at one time there had been something on there, at some time there had been the bustle of daily life in this emptiness. But, even the remains of the house that this fireplace had once warmed had turned to dust and dirt. Just the sandstone hearth, the rectangular void where the fire was built, and the chimney reaching toward the sky remained.

Tommy and his father had gone that morning to remove the only monument that remained. Jack brought the backhoe off the trailer and lifted the bucket as high as it would go, positioning it in such a way that he could swing the bucket around, hit the front side of the chimney, and push it back the ground. Then Jack intended to scoop the loose fallen stone with the bucket and load it on the truck. Tommy stood clear as the backhoe took its first blow. Six or eight feet of the chimney waved back and forth in the sunlight before it succumbed to the ground below. His father lowered the bucket and bought it around again to strike the second blow. This time, Tommy continued with the excitement of a small child, and the second blow brought the entire chimney down leaving only the firebox and the hearth behind.

While his father repositioned to load what had fallen to the ground, Tommy stepped upon the hearth and looked into the square hole where the fireplace became a chimney and began its upward climb. It was on a ledge inside the fireplace that Tommy found the woman's cameo brooch and a pair gloves. Until Jack pushed the chimney to the ground, that hidden ledge was *inside* the fireplace. In order to place the brooch and gloves there one would have to reach up inside the fireplace and place the items there with a purpose. The

5

brooch and gloves were only revealed because of Jack's backhoe. Had Tommy not stepped upon the fireplace hearth to look in the firebox, the brooch and gloves would have succumbed to the final blow of the backhoe and no doubt been lost forever. Each was old long before they were hidden in the fireplace and time had taken its toll. The cameo brooch had tarnished in the extremes of heat and cold. The delicate stitching around the fingers of the gloves was rotted and frayed due to exposure. Of course, the fireplace had no doubt offered some protection from time and the elements.

Both items, the gloves, and the brooch were still very much intact. Tommy brought them to me knowing my passion for the old and forgotten. Tommy and Bobby both spent hours of their youths with me sweeping a metal detector over vacant lots and country fields, looking for threads of the past that might supply insight into the future. This searching for clues from the past was strictly a hobby for me but also felt like an obsession how the earth drew me to discover what lay beneath it in places richly steeped in history. My collection is comprised of one hundred items worth nothing, four or five worth something, and the one rusted pocket watch and chain that might be of value if it still had hands and numbers on the face.

The two prizes Tommy had brought to share with me would no doubt send the value of my collection skyrocketing, if only they were mine, and Tommy offered them. I accepted them only on the condition that they would always be his, but I gladly would jump at the chance to investigate their origin. On that note, we struck a deal that would reveal to us something more horrible, more horrendous, and more shocking than we could have ever dreamed, and bring us closer than any father and son could ever be.

2

I TOOK THE BROOCH AND THE GLOVES TO THE TABLE
in the garage reserved for my relics. Mounted to the left was a large
lighted magnifying glass mounted on a movable arm. The glass could
be positioned up and down for focusing. I carefully examined the
gloves under the glass and discovered nothing remarkable. They were
small, reddish-brown, with a slight ruffling at the wrist of each.
Curiously, neither appeared to suffer any effects of a fire, the obvious
conclusion is that they had been placed there on the ledge inside the
fireplace after its use had ceased. Inside the gloves, where they had
been folded together, they were still a deep red. Rain had inevitably
found its way down the chimney to the outer surfaces and faded
them to the point that they appeared to be two different colors when
opened. I probed carefully inside the gloves for a mark that might
reveal either their place of origin, the maker of the gloves, or maybe
even their owner. If such a message had existed, time had washed it
away long ago.

The cameo brooch was not in as good a state as the gloves. It
would seem it should have better weathered the strains of time, but
the profile of a woman etched in the stone was just a shadow, a
change from dark to light across its surface. In tiny crevices, the small
ups and downs in the stone, there were flashes of green that would
probably prove to be alive if viewed under a microscope. The frame
around the stone was ornate, but just as the stone, impossible to tell
of what it was made. It, too, was encrusted with time and
microscopic plant life.

The back of the cameo was smoother and slightly less crusted over. Under the magnifying glass, there were three dark areas that descended like stair steps from left to right. I was hopeful that these tiny spots were initials, but the entire surface of the stone was only an inch and a half long and an inch wide. Cleaning away enough of the crust that held so tightly to it to read the letters would be painstaking, cautious work. I doubted my own amateur skills with such a timely prize from the past as this, but I knew just whom to take it to and would do so as soon as possible.

I placed both the gloves and the brooch in separate plastic bags and then placed each of the bags in a wooden box I kept for transporting the small, sometimes indistinguishable, items I had collected over the years. Of course, never had I possessed such bounty as this. Nor did I have a piece that so fascinated my senses. I had jars of musket balls, a rusted flintlock from a black powder rifle, a bayonet, and even the handle and six inches of an officer's saber, but none held any mystery. The Civil War raged across the river here one hundred and thirty years ago. All these were explainable remnants of battles lost and won. Even the pocket watch with the eroded numbers and displaced hands held no conspiracy. I found it in the dust of a cotton field, no doubt lost and plowed under time and time again until my metal detector sensed it hidden in the dirt. To find a woman's brooch and gloves purposely concealed, prized possessions hidden away and discovered so long after the fact, would surely tell a different tale than my other finds. Who had hidden the gloves and brooch in such a place? What was so mysterious about the two items that they needed to be hidden from sight?

I went in and called Tommy to see if he wanted to ride the next day to a jeweler who might tell us something about the brooch. Jack and I spoke only briefly after he told me Tommy wasn't in. I asked him to tell Tommy to call me and he cordially, but reluctantly, said he would.

Jack Morrow and I had long been acquaintances, mostly out of responsibility to our sons. We stopped on the street and talked, but only out of common courtesy. As Bobby and Tommy grew up, Jack

8

and I often sat next to each other at school functions and we talked on the phone when necessary, but Jack and I never really *liked* each other. Jack, I believed, disliked me more than I disliked him. It was a matter of attitude and outlook toward life. We had known each other in high school, but we were not friends then either. After college, I returned here to become a personnel manager at one of the dozen or so industries that dotted the banks of the river. I was eventually promoted to head of personnel. I had a good life, made a respectable upper-middle-class income and had my weekends and holidays off. I, Bobby's mother, Mary, and our two younger daughters, Ashley and Sarah, had lived a comfortable, unobtrusive, admittedly somewhat mundane life. We had a minivan in the driveway, a camper parked beside the garage, and a small in-ground pool in the backyard.

My job and all these memorials to leisure time were constant thorns in Jack Morrow's side. Jack was of a school and background that dictated if one was awake, one was supposed to be working, or at least thinking about working. To have a hobby, such as my constant detecting and digging in the dirt for pieces of the past, was too much for him to bear.

Tommy had spent most of his youth doing something six days a week that in his father's eyes compared to work. He did have Sunday afternoons off if he had finished what he started on Saturday. He was never allowed to dream, which is where I believe Jack's internal conflict with me arose. When Tommy was with Bobby and me, not only did I allow him to dream, I encouraged it. Bobby, Tommy, and I spent many free-time hours over the years digging in the dirt hoping for a pot of gold. We never found it, but all we really needed was the dream that it might be there.

In this respect, I think Tommy was more like me than Bobby. There was genuine excitement in his eyes as he dug feverishly in the dirt for these fragments that were only a treasure in the eyes of their beholder. Every piece I offered to Tommy over the years he refused, knowing that to his father it would just be a rusty piece of metal that needed to either be repaired to a state of usefulness or thrown out. Sometimes now I look back and wonder if Tommy was as much

Bobby's friend as he was my protégé. I think now that Tommy's escape from his father was in reality, perhaps more important than his friendship with Bobby. That's why Tommy hid the brooch and gloves until he could bring them to me. He didn't tell me his father hadn't seen them, but I know he hadn't. If he had, he would have instructed Tommy to throw them on the truck with the rest of the scrap.

In retrospect, I wondered if I should have called and given his father a reason to believe Tommy was dreaming again. After all, I was sure his father would be even harder on Tommy now. In Jack's eyes, whatever excuses he could make for Tommy's dreaming as a boy no longer held true. For a man like Jack Morrow, whatever unrealistic dreams of buried treasure and lost legends beneath the dirt Tommy had as a boy, should have come to an end on his eighteenth birthday.

Tommy returned my call about 9:30 that night. I told him I was going to take the brooch to a jeweler I knew in Springhill who specialized in antique jewelry. Tommy asked me to hold on; he was away from the phone for only eight or ten seconds when he returned. Tommy apologized and thanked me for asking him along but said he and his father had to work. I volunteered that I would wait until Tommy could go if he preferred, but he immediately said for me to go on without him, saying he'd stop by and see what I found out as soon as he could. He was gone from the phone such a short time I don't really know if he had even asked his father for permission to go with me. He knew his father's answer as well as I did. Tommy was going to have to take more control of his life at some point, but this was a subject of which I would need to steer clear. Jack Morrow already suspected I was responsible for his son's lack of interest in their business; I didn't want to be the cause of his total rebellion.

I sat down at the kitchen table to examine the brooch one more time. As I turned it over in my hands, I decided I'd better go this one alone. Although the brooch and gloves belonged to Tommy, he had turned them over to me. I believed there was implied consent for me to do with them whatever I felt was best. Besides, his father's attitude would make Tommy's participation next to impossible, at least not without a fight. I really did not want to be the cause of that rift between father and son. It would, no doubt, come of its own accord someday without my help. I decided then that I would just let Tommy find out what he wanted to at his own pace.

I left Saturday morning at 8:00 a.m. for Springhill. It was, to the best of my recollection, about an hour's drive. I hadn't been there since I had taken in the pocket watch five years before. I was almost there when it occurred to me that I should have called first. The little old man who owned the shop was *very* old five years ago. As Springhill came into sight, I realized that there was a definite possibility that neither he nor the shop would be there. Too late now, just as well to drive by and see. I had a very clear picture of the old man in my mind as I turned toward the downtown business district. Small and frail, grey hair, very sparse on the sides no hair on the top of his head, an ill-shaped grey beard that would have served him much better had it been worn on the top of his head, he wore baggy black pants and a flannel shirt a size or two too large. My most vivid memory was of the two pairs of glasses he wore. One pair on his nose, half-lenses, like reading glasses. The other pair was perched on the top of his head. This was a pair of jewelers' glasses, the kind that has a smaller lens mounted in an arm that swings up and down. This pair had two arms, one on either side. He was very friendly and talkative. He introduced himself the minute I opened the door.

Abraham Oppenheim had been honest and sincere when I took the pocket watch to him. He hadn't needed his jeweler's glasses to tell me that at one time, a long time ago, this was a nice watch. Mr. Oppenheim had said with a heaviness in his voice, "It is a watch only the man who took it from the ground can cherish now." He patted me on the shoulder as he told me, as if to counsel, stating in the kindest way he knew that is was just a piece of junk. Of course, it was the information that he gave me after the letdown that brought me back here with the brooch.

He told me the watch was made in Germany, before 'our' Civil War. He told me it was gold and had, at one time, had a cut glass crystal face and very elaborate hands. He even pulled down a dusty catalog and showed me a picture of what the watch probably looked like before it ended up under a foot of dirt. I felt certain as I rounded the corner toward his shop that if anybody could tell me about this brooch he could. He'd probably have a picture to go with it. Of course, this was all dependent on whether he had survived the last five years. I was about to find out if he had.

3

I PULLED UP IN FRONT OF OPPENHEIM JEWELRY. There was plenty of parking, maybe four or five cars up and down the street. This was obviously the old business district of Springhill with dilapidated buildings two and three stories high. The stores were faded, and the lettering along the brick surfaces was illegible in its cracked, peeling state. Even the sidewalks were cracking and in need of repair. Oppenheim's was no exception. His storefront was like the others. One of the panes of glass had been cracked diagonally along its surface and had been carefully repaired with wide duct tape to prevent the wind from dislodging it from its frame.

I stepped across the brittle sidewalk and gently swung the door open, afraid pushing it too hard lest it separate from its hinges. I saw Mr. Oppenheim off to my right sitting on a stool, bent over his workbench. The warmness in his voice had not changed.

"Abraham Oppenheim here, be with you in a minute," he called. He didn't stop what he was doing, never straightened his back, only gave a friendly greeting as he did five years ago to every customer that crossed the threshold.

I looked around at the jewelry and watches in the dusty display cases as he continued to work. He sighed heavily and spoke, I believe to himself stating, "Maybe it can't be fixed." He laid the watch he was working on down on his table and swiveled the seat of his stool around toward me. He raised his jeweler's glasses up and pulled his reading glasses down to his eyes before he spoke. When he did, I know my mouth dropped even though I didn't feel it.

"My friend," he said with a broad smile on his bearded face, "have you found another watch in the ground?"

I was utterly amazed and I stared for a moment before I spoke. "You remember me?"

He responded by stating, "What – maybe four or five years ago?" The German in his accent was especially pronounced when he said the word years. "No, my mind is still pretty clear," he laughed. "I keep expecting it to go any day, but so far I can remember."

I had not meant to imply senility, but he had not taken offense. He looked the same, no older, no younger. I think he was wearing the same pants and shirt as before. The only difference I noticed in his dress was the rubber bands he had installed high up on his arms to keep his sleeves off his hands..

I answered his question stating, "No watch this time; I have a brooch I'd like for you to look at."

I had removed the brooch from the wooden box before I left that morning, bringing only it and leaving the gloves behind. I wondered to myself if I should have brought them. With a mind as sharp as his, he may have been able to tell me the year they were made, even though it was not his area of expertise. I took the brooch from my pocket, still in the same plastic bag, and laid it on the glass counter. He reached for it and turned it over in his hands several times before he removed it from the bag. He changed his glasses out again and looked at both sides through his jeweler's glasses before he spoke.

"Older than a hundred, I suspect. We'll have to put it in some acid before we can tell." He flipped the brooch over a few more times in his hands and said, "I don't think we can restore it like it was," with an apologetic tone in his voice, "but the acid will tell us a lot about the lady's face."

I reached and turned it over in his hands and asked him if he thought there were initials on the back. He brought down the small lens on the left side of his glasses and moved the back of the brooch close to his face.

"Maybe a jeweler's mark; sometimes they did that." He took the brooch and moved behind the counter to a room with velvet curtains for a door. From behind the curtain, he beckoned me to come back.

The back of the store was worse than the front with dusty shelves stuffed to overflowing. A rickety staircase ascended to the second floor. It too was stacked with boxes and books. There was space on each step about the size of two feet side-by-side. To the right of the curtain, sat another workbench. It, too, was stacked full. Enough room had been left on the table for three small rectangular ceramic tubs about five inches deep. Mr. Oppenheim took a pair of tongs and carefully lowered the brooch into the first tub on his right. The liquid began to bubble. I assumed it was acid and was curious, but I didn't ask, afraid I might offend. Besides, if the liquid would hurt the brooch, it was too late now. He removed the brooch several times with the tongs and looked at it before it took it out and lowered it into the second tub. He appeared to be counting to himself as he watched it fizz and bubble, less so in this tub than the first. Finally, he removed the brooch from the second tub and moved it back and forth in the third as if to wash it. The third tub didn't fizz or bubble, but steam or smoke appeared to rise from it as the brooch was pushed back and forth with the tongs.

"They don't make these chemicals anymore," he said, "I don't know what I'll do when these are gone."

I looked to the left of the staircase and saw several barrels with large skulls and crossbones etched across their circumferences. I see on the news occasionally where health officials are removing abandoned toxic waste barrels. I thought to myself I'd no doubt be reading about a chemical removal at Oppenheim Jewelers when he dies. I could count five barrels from where I was standing, and there were more behind those. Mr. Oppenheim was very optimistic about his life expectancy if he was afraid of using up his supply. I breathed a little shallow, wondering if I stood too close as the brooch bubbled in the tub, but, after all, Mr. Oppenheim had his face right over the tubs and seemed no worse for wear. I wondered for just a minute if standing over these acid tubs explained the sharpness of his mind, but the timeworn look of his body. Maybe he was really fifty, but the acid had aged him to look like he was ninety. I abandoned the thought when I heard him say, "Ah! There we are, the lady is Greek."

4

AS HE SPOKE, I WAS IN SORT OF A DAZE, GOING BACK and forth in my mind between his age and the acid barrels in the back.

"I'm sorry, I didn't understand," I said.

Mr. Oppenheim patiently repeated, "The lady on the cameo is Greek." He was moving through the velvet door curtains, back to the front of the stores as he spoke. "Come; we need to see her in the light." Mr. Oppenheim moved quickly to his workbench in the front of the store. He sat on his stool and began rummaging through the shelves that overlooked the work surface. "Ah, there they are," he stated, motioning me to come closer handing me a second pair of jeweler's glasses. "Put those on and we'll see what she looks like."

He handed me the glasses and a rag, since the glasses had as much dust on them as the rest of the store. I cleaned all four lenses as Mr. Oppenheim brought his work light closer to the brooch. He motioned me beside him and began to talk. He had picked up a small file to use as a pointer.

"This lady has a wing over her right ear that extends beyond her head. Her hair is long and looks like snakes. Medusa, a Greek goddess," he said in a high-pitched and frenzied voice, unlike any I had heard him speak previously. He went on, "Made in the mid-eighteen hundreds, in Idar-Oberstein, Germany. The stone is Sardonyx. The craftsman who did this was very talented. His work is good under the glasses and the light."

He handed me the brooch and offered me his seat as he disappeared back behind the velvet curtain. The stone was a brown and white mix when viewed up close. Even with my limited

16

knowledge I could see the detail in the stonework was exquisite. The profile of the woman's head was so precise it was hard to imagine the tools that made the lines in her face, let alone the hands guiding them. Mr. Oppenheim returned from the back with a dusty catalog. He had already opened it to the page with a drawing of the cameo.

"I missed the time period." The high pitch had disappeared from his voice. "But the place was right; Idar-Oberstein, as I said. Produced between 1805 and 1815. It was not sold in the United States." Before I could tell him that I didn't understand, he continued to talk as he looked at the catalog, stating, "this lady came here either in possession of a European who brought it here or was purchased by an American while he or she was in Europe."

I wondered how he could know all of this from one catalog. Then, there was the wealth of information he apparently retains in his head. Clearly, I could not dispute him.

I had already forgotten about the letters on the back. While he continued to thumb through his catalog, I turned the brooch over with the anticipation of a child waiting for a shot in the arm. I almost wanted to close my eyes as the back came into view of the glasses and the light. There were letters there and they were very legible! R.L.G. descended from left to right. I read them out loud. I had almost forgotten in my fervor to see the letters that Mr. Oppenheim was there.

"That is not the fashion in which the craftsman would have marked his work. It is one of the owner's initials." One of the owners! "You must understand," he said in almost a monotone, "the brooch is very old. It could have changed hands many times; these could be the initials of anyone who had owned this stone in these many many years."

I had not thought of that. I was disappointed when I thought that these letters might lead to nothing but frustration.

"I will tell you something else, but it may only confuse you more." I had not realized I was confused. Mr. Oppenheim went on. "Somewhere there is a pair of earrings that came with this piece." He moved toward the table and picked up the file he had been using for a pointer, and then pulled his glasses down to look at the brooch. "You see these projections on either side of the setting?" He was pointing to the ornate frame around the stone. "They were made about half-way down the length of the brooch on either side. These projections were used to attach the earrings when the jewelry was put away, so they would not become separated." He took the end of the file and turned the pin over in my hands. "Also, there was a chain to go with it. These tiny protrusions at the top of the frame are where an eyelet existed for the chain to go through, so the brooch could be worn as a necklace. It was long ago broken off." He continued in that apologetic tone he had used to inform me that my pocket watch was junk stating, "Of course, any of the pieces could have been separated from each other at any time, or they might be in the same place you found the brooch if you look again."

I envisioned the chimney where Tommy found the brooch falling to the ground and being scooped up by his father's backhoe. With that picture came an incredible urge to get back to Oakman. I restrained myself as I removed the jewelers' glasses from my nose and stood to tell Mr. Oppenheim goodbye.

"How much do I owe you for your time?"

Mr. Oppenheim responded, "Time is very cheap." He looked past me as he stroked his white beard. "Shall we say two dollars?" He continued while I reached for my wallet. "You should pay me five and keep the glasses. I think you will wish you had them when you look at the brooch again."

I hesitated as I looked in my wallet, wondering if I really didn't owe him a lot more. "Are you sure five dollars is enough? You wasted your entire morning with me."

He laughed. "And as you can see, I've lost a lot of customers while you were here."

I handed him the five dollars and turned to return the brooch to the plastic bag. I started to ask him again if he was sure five dollars was enough when a customer came in the door.

"Abraham Oppenheim here, be with you in a moment," he said as he waved at the woman coming through the door. He patted me on the back as I walked around the counter and told me to come back any time stating, "I hope what you are looking for is there in the earth. Perhaps you have just not yet discovered exactly where to look!"

As I walked back onto the cracked sidewalk. I heard him ask the woman who came in, "How may I help you?" just as the rickety door of the shop closed behind me.

5

I DO NOT REMEMBER THE TRIP BACK HOME. I DROVE fast, my mind on the earrings. What possible difference could it make if I did find them? They would just be another piece of the puzzle that I could not solve. The letters, 'R.L.G.' flashed back and forth, too. I even tried stupidly to switch the letters around in my head; this wouldn't help, but it passed the time as I continued home. I tried to think of names that started with R such as Renee, Robin, Rebecca. I also thought I really did not know how much names had changed in the last 180 years. Through it all, I could remember Mr. Oppenheim saying the brooch was very old and could have changed hands several times, many times. This was true, so even if the brooch had a name on it, that would be no guarantee that this name had anything to do with the owner I was now convinced I had to find.

The brooch was beginning to exert some control over me. It was the brooch and its origin that were driving me back home, consuming my thoughts. I had forgotten the time and the day, and I was oblivious to houses and barns passing by my window as I drove toward Oakman. I arrived home and pulled up in my driveway before I knew it. I didn't even remember coming into town, let alone turning and winding through the streets to my house. I scrambled out of the car, leaving the door open and the motor running. I feverishly ran into the garage and grabbed my metal detector, returned to the car and backed out of the driveway. If Mary had known I had come and gone, I was not aware of it. I think, for those moments, I did not even care. Getting to Penn Road and findings those earrings was all-consuming.

As with the trip back from Springhill, I do not remember driving to Penn Road. I only vaguely remember running the two or three

20

hundred yards to the site where the chimney had been before Jack Morrow had scraped it from the ground and took it away in his truck. I thought about that truck and Jack Morrow, childishly hating him for a moment. He most likely had hauled away the rest of my puzzle. He removed it in a couple of hours; a secret hidden for perhaps a century, and for a few seconds in time I hated him for it.

Jack disappeared from my mind as the metal detector began to signal the vastness of the metal below the surface of the ground. I had forgotten the collapsible shovel I usually carry for digging, but it did not matter. I picked up a rock and scraped away dirt from several of the objects to which the detector had alerted me: a rusty door hinge, a barrel ring from an old wooden keg, nails everywhere, half of a dog-iron from a fireplace. The farther I moved away from the site of the old chimney, the more the detector beeped! It hummed in an almost constant scream that there was metal everywhere. I was about half-way back the distance to Penn Road when I began to realize it was getting dark.

Somewhere in my subconsciousness, I recalled the ground under my feet as I ran to the site of the old chimney was different from the fields I had searched before. There was a roughness, an unevenness to the ground my legs had not experienced previously. I rationalized momentarily that it was the running that caused the sensation under my feet, but now, as I ambled back toward Penn Road, I realized what I missed before. I turned my metal detector off and raised my head as the sun began to set in front of me. I turned around in a circle and surveyed the open field in the light of the setting sun. Everywhere, in every direction, there was a glistening of light as the setting sun illuminated this small part of the world as it did at no other time of the day. An old wagon wheel protruded slightly from the ground off to my right. I walked over to a washtub turned upside down and barely exposed to the eye. The sun bounced and danced off pieces of glass in every direction glittering like fire on the surface of the uneven ground.

There had not been only one house at this site, but many, an entire community up and down Penn Road along the railroad tracks.

Many beyond the last remaining chimney had existed at one time on this site. In the setting sun, I could even see the remains of the streets and alleys that came and went around the houses, the thruways that linked this community with Penn Road and the rest of Oakman.

As I aimlessly walked back to my car, I realized it was parked in the middle of the road. I put the metal detector on the back seat and turned to look one more time as the sun slowly disappeared in the distance. It was only then that I realized that the brooch was only a tiny piece of this puzzle. I spent nearly my whole life here and never once had known. Never once had anybody said there used to be a whole settlement of people here living in the houses that had so long ago returned to the earth! There was a secret concealed here and the brooch in my pocket was only a small part of it.

I took the brooch out and looked at it once more as the last rays of the light faded. The lady who wore this brooch could probably tell me the secret, but she was probably long since dead and gone. Whoever hid the brooch and the gloves in the chimney could tell me, but there was no reason to believe they might still be alive, either. And I had no way of knowing that they were not one in the same, yet my gut told me they were not.

The need to know was so much more compelling now than it had been when the brooch was all I had. The need to know these people and their fate overshadowed everything as I sat down in my car. I realized as I returned home that I was dirty from digging in the dirt there on Penn Road. I had been down on my knees several times looking for an answer. I had not realized that there were questions in every direction in that open field on Penn Road. I suspected the answers were someplace else.

I pulled into my driveway and turned the car off, throwing my head back on the headrest. I felt like I had been awake for a week. I closed my eyes and recalled that open field one more time when the silence was broken outside my car window.

"Mr. Wallace, are you all right? You look like you've been in a fight!" It was Tommy, he'd come by to ask about the brooch. God knows I had a lot to tell him.

6

TOMMY STAYED UNTIL ABOUT NINE-THIRTY. I TOLD him what Mr. Oppenheim said about the brooch, my discovery on Penn Road, and everything I knew so far. Tommy stared on cautiously while I spoke, never saying a word. I think he thought I lost my mind just a little. Here I sat, filthy and dirty from head-to-toe, rambling about a place and people who, it appeared to Tommy, did not and probably had never existed. Somehow, through it all, I tied the brooch to that place time and time again. That undoubtedly made my story even harder to believe. Tommy patiently listened until I was completely finished before he spoke.

"I have never heard of a whole community there on Penn Road, Mr. Wallace, just the one house where we tore the chimney down."

That was the point exactly! No one had ever heard of a settlement there, and someone surely must have known it existed. I made that point repeatedly throughout my conversation with Tommy, but I was never sure he understood. A multitude of people had come and gone there on Penn Road, and apparently, no one remembered that it had ever been occupied. These unknown souls and the homes they lived in were merely allowed to be covered by time, hidden away from sight and mind. One house or two and an old barn abandoned on a country road were familiar sights. Even dilapidated houses waiting to be razed by the city in need of a place to progress. This was something different. These houses and their inhabitants had been removed conspicuously and purposely from sight and memory.

I asked Tommy as he was leaving, to ask his father and anyone else he knew what had been there, and who had lived there on Penn

Road. In my mind, I felt Jack Morrow did not know any more about Penn Road than I did. After all, we had grown up together, and there was the just a one-year difference in our ages. There was little reason for him to have more information about what went on there than I did. I thought hard about who might know. I searched my brain for the oldest person I knew in town who had lived here all his or her life. I realized as I pondered, I simply did not know that many older people, at least, not any really older people.

Finally, I thought of Mr. Humphries who owned a store in town, the only one of its kind left. A sort of general store down by the railroad tracks that sold a little bit of everything. Clothing, tools, garden seed, groceries, just everything. The hand-painted letters on the front windows still read, "Humphries' Dry Goods." Mr. Humphries was old, how old I was not quite sure. You could find him any day of the week, except Sunday, sitting in his rocker in the middle of the store by an old pot-belly stove. He had looked old as long as I could remember. Grey-headed, always wearing a hat and denim railroad coat. I could see his shoes quite vividly: quarter-high boots with an elastic band on each side. I can remember going with my father to the store when I was a child, usually to buy tools, and thinking Mr. Humphries boots looked very much like a picture of Robin Hood I had seen in a book. Quarter-high and pointed at the end. I am sure they were not as pointed as I remember as a child, and Mr. Humphries had never been a candidate for one of Robin Hood's Merry Men. In all the times I had gone into the store as a child, I could never remember him moving out of his chair. He would say, "Just help yourself!" It was his wife, Mrs. Humphries, who appeared from the shelves to wait on customers. It was she who went to the cash register to check the customers out. Then, as you left, Mr. Humphries would wave and say, "Come back soon, tell your friends and relations we're here!"

Looking back, I don't really know if Mr. Humphries can walk. When his wife died several years ago, his daughter took over her mother's place, and routine perpetuated itself. The only real change in Mr. Humphries' life in the last twenty-five years was that he switched his tobacco habit from a pipe to snuff. The only other change is that for the last ten years or so, he has been continually wiping his cheek with a handkerchief where the snuff runs down his face. Other than this, the scene remains the same. His daughter even looks like her mother, so for anyone who only goes into his store every four or five years, no change appears to have occurred at all.

Six months ago, Mr. Humphries was still sitting in his chair, I had gone in and bought a pair of coveralls to wear to go digging. He was definitely my man! I could see something on the front door of the store that said, "Since 1900 something". As many times as I had gone through that door in my lifetime, I could not remember just exactly what the year was. May 1915 ? I was not sure.

Tomorrow was Sunday, so it would be Monday before I could see him. I had calmed down. I no longer felt the urgency I experienced before. I wanted to know what had happened on Penn Road, but, after all, my life would have to go on. I would no doubt be at it for a long time connecting the brooch to its owner, if I could locate her at all. In the meantime, Mr. Humphries may not be as old as the missing residents of Penn Road, but for the time being, I suspected he was as close as I was going to get.

I really did not do anything on Sunday. I had seen what there was to see on Penn Road. I spent part of the day making up names for the initials 'R.L.G.' again, but otherwise, I wasted a lot of time. I started out toward the field on Penn road several times, but decided I needed to be armed with something more. A name, a year, just something more, so that I might have a more precise look. I did try to think of what I would do next if Mr. Humphries failed me. I knew the library had old *Oakman Sentinels* on microfilm. I had never used them, but heard Bobby talk about using them to do various reports in high school. Unfortunately, I had no idea how old the *Sentinel* was. I could remember in my lifetime, when it changed from a weekly to a daily newspaper, I must have been around ten or eleven years old.

No matter how far back they might go, I still needed a date, month, or year, a starting point to begin my search. Even with that, there was no guarantee the paper had reported this event. Even now, the *Sentinel* was not famous for reporting bad things that happened in town; depending entirely on who the bad news was about.

I fell asleep on the couch rehearsing what I would say to Mr. Humphries tomorrow. I had never carried on a conversation with him. I had to find the right words to ask him if he was old enough to remember what, if anything, had happened on Penn Road. I had to at least ask him if anyone had ever lived there during his lifetime. I guessed there was nothing to do except just come right out and ask.

7

I WENT TO WORK EARLY AND SPENT THE MORNING rehearsing what I would say to Mr. Humphries instead of working. I could have taken the morning off, I had plenty of leave time coming to me, but I rationalized that my life could not stop to pursue what was quickly becoming an obsession. I sat at my desk and acted like I was busy as I made up a list of questions in my head for Mr. Humphries right up until noon. I left work and drove downtown, hoping upon hope Mr. Humphries could tell me all I wanted to know. In the back of my mind, I hoped he would tell me a story about a brooch that disappeared on Penn Road and the name of the woman who lost it, but I knew nothing could be that easy.

I parked, and from across the street, could see Mr. Humphries through the glass door. From this view, nothing seemed changed. As I waited for cars to pass, I could see him sitting there in his chair just as always. I crossed the street and went in the front door of the store receiving the usual greeting.

"Come in, just help yourself." His arms moving in the same fashion as always. He continued and said, "My daughter, Arvada, is in the store somewhere. She'll help you find whatever you need."

I was standing directly in front of him almost toe-to-toe before I spoke again. Obviously, he was afraid he might be in jeopardy of having to move. I said, "Actually, I wanted to talk to you, Mr. Humphries." He stared at me with a little snuff running down his right cheek, with a look of slight amazement. After a pause that seemed to last five minutes, he spoke in a kind of deep wet voice.

"Well then, have a seat, talking is free."

Mr. Humphries motioned me to the rocking chair beside him

27

and I sat down cautiously looking for snuff stains on the chair. Then again, I'm pretty sure he never sits in the chair he offered me. He spat in a coffee can he kept wedged between the chair and his right leg and seemed genuinely happy I stopped to talk. I noted the stains on the leg of his overalls where it appeared he more than often missed the can. For a second, I thought I would move my chair to his left side, so I would be out of the line of fire, but it probably would not have helped; he would have just moved the can. When he smiled, I could see his lips were stained reddish-brown from the snuff. He spat toward the can by his leg, and I could see for a moment he had only had about two teeth. I surveyed him for a second or two to see if everything was in place. Hat still on his head, tilted to the right as always. His overalls appeared new except for the snuff stain on the right leg. His railroad jacket was old and faded, the point of the collar on his ride side more testimony to his habit of dipping snuff. It was stained by what ran down his cheek in between wipes with the blue and white handkerchief he kept in the bib pocket of his overalls. I looked down at his feet with caution. His elastic and leather shoes were just as I remembered. However, they were not nearly as pointed as I recalled from my childhood.

"How can I help you?" He smiled again, and a little snuff rolled down his cheek.

I asked, "Have you lived here all your life, Mr. Humphries?"

He responded, "Yes, sir, all eighty-four years of it." He was old; that was good, but I was really hoping for ninety-four.

"I was wondering if you could tell me what used to be out on Penn Road, there in that open field?"

He seemed to honestly study my question for a minute before he answered by stating, "Nothing."

I questioned, "You mean there was never anything there?"

He seemed to have to think again before he answered, "Well sir, not in my lifetime, nothing but a lot of stone, but people moved it over the years."

"Stone, I do not understand."

He responded, "Lots of foundation and fireplace stone, Must

have been houses there at one time. People went in there with wagons and moved the stones to use for piers and fireplaces for other houses."

"Do you know who lived there when there were houses?"

This time he leaned his head back and looked at the ceiling. He got strangled on some snuff that rolled down his throat and had to cough it up before he could speak.

"Before my time, but I believe those were quarters down there."

"Quarters?"

He answered by stating, "Colored people. I believe that's where they lived back then."

I had to stop and think for a minute before I could go on. It had never occurred to me that this was the Black section of town at that time. And it still did not tell me where they had gone and why.

"Do you know where they all went?"

He responded, "No, can't say that I do. The Black section has always been over there by the river. Leastways all my life."

"Did you ever hear what happened to all the houses? Did anyone ever say why they were gone?"

"No sir, not as I recall. You must work for the city. I heard they was building down there. Y'all got some kinda land dispute? Ain't that just like the city – own something ninety years and still not know if it belongs to them."

I did not answer the question about working for the city. What would be the point? There was no way I could explain why I wanted to know about the people who lived there on Penn Road.

I got up, reached to shake Mr. Humphries' hand, and thanked him. He wiped the snuff from his mouth and offered me his hand as he spat in the coffee can one more time.

"I hope I helped you out. Lord, you'd think the city would have known what used to be down there."

I told him he was a big help as I turned to walk toward the door. As I opened it, I heard him say over my shoulder, "Come back soon, tell your friends and relations we're here."

When I got back in my car and sat down. I was immersed in the thought that Mr. Humphries had said he was eighty-four years old and that there was nothing on Penn Road but some stone. Whatever had gone on there in that field happened perhaps ninety or even a hundred years ago. He had not given me much, but it was certainly a place to start. I sat in my car in a daze reviewing the knowns. The brooch, the open field, the 'colored section.' Again, I tried to put names with the inscription on the brooch. I rolled the facts around in my head repeating them silently. Time passed as my thoughts morphed into a dreamlike state.

My eyes wandered up the street to the newly erected bank clock that read 1:34 p.m. I started the car and moved away from the curb. My hour for lunch had passed thirty-four minutes ago. The obsession had taken hold and was exponentially growing.

When I arrived home that afternoon, Mary was sitting at the kitchen table sipping a cup of coffee. I knew from twenty-three years of marriage that she knew something was wrong. She looked over her coffee cup and asked me about my day. I felt certain that someone had called her when I did not return to work on time. Now all she knew was that I had done something completely out of character, and I could tell by the look on her face that she wanted to know what it was. I am quite sure she had sat there at the table after she received the call telling her I was missing in action and imagined all sorts of thing. After all, I was forty-five years old. Up until now, the mid-life crisis had passed me by, but she could have easily imagined that it had caught up with me. I had not realized it, but I had spent the entire weekend in a kind of self-indulged trance. I had answered either yes, no, or uh huh to every question. Ever since Tommy had brought the brooch to me, I slipped in and out of the garage or spent the rest of my time on the living room couch away from Mary and the girls. I had left Saturday morning, stayed most of the day, come home, left again without explanation, then returned to the living room couch. Through it all, I had never once said or explained anything to Mary.

Sunday was the same. I spent the day purposely avoiding contact with Mary or the girls, afraid of having to explain. Always touching the brooch, whether it was in my hand or holding it in my pocket, I kept the brooch close. Holding it in my hand when I was alone, putting it in my pocket when I heard someone coming, but continuing to hold on to it out of sight. I never once stopped to tell Mary why. My strange behavior on the weekend, coupled with the totally out of character incident at work, had now sent Mary's mind reeling, and rightfully so. She had no doubt sat there at the table and imagined everything from a torrid affair that ran over my lunch hour to my demise in a red sports car I really did not know how to drive. Whatever she had imagined, I deserved. We had a good marriage, we had always been able to talk, and this should have been no exception. Now, as she lowered her coffee cup to the table, I knew she was waiting for the explanation she deserved.

I had to backtrack in my mind for a moment to recall the question she had asked when I came in the door: how had my day gone, or been, something like that. It was said with a tone that let me know she had at least some partial pieces of information. There was no reason for me to not tell her. In fact, she would probably be a big help. After all, she had been my partner in the digs before Bobby and Tommy. Mary was the one who bought me the metal detector. I could not explain to myself why I had forgotten all of that, how I had not remembered that Mary was my best ally. I had told her every secret I had to tell in the last twenty-three or -four years. What had caused me to lock her out this time? I did not know. I felt a little ashamed that I was afraid of sharing my prize with anyone, even Mary. I had even had those feelings toward Tommy on Saturday as I explained to him what Mr. Oppenheim had said about the brooch.

I sighed as I sat down at the table and answered her question with, "not too good. I got tied up downtown with Mr. Humphries. I was nearly an hour late getting back to work." I restrained from telling her I daydreamed an hour in the car. There was almost a smile on her face as I continued. Mr. Humphries was not the diversion she had pictured in her mind.

"Mr. Humphries? What could you possibly have to say that would hold you spellbound for one and a half hours with Mr.

Humphries?" She was thrilled I was not having an affair, but she was equally as confounded that I had been distracted by a somewhat grubby, snuff-dipping, toothless old man. I think she was trying to remember, as I had if he could carry on a conversation.

Now I had no choice but to show her the brooch, tell her about Penn Road, and hope that she would be my confidante in this as she had been in other somewhat useless endeavors. Her tone had changed from relief to perturbation in those brief seconds. In all our years as husband and wife, I had never gone so far off the path. I had been late for work perhaps five times in the past twenty years. On each occasion, I had a viable excuse and had not only called the plant but Mary as well. She knew this was different from just digging in the dirt on Sunday afternoon. She knew I had always been able to separate my hobby from the realities of life and she undoubtedly felt the obsession in my voice, although I did not try to hide it.

I took the brooch out of my pocket and laid it on the table for her inspection. I started at the beginning and worked through to the present, trying to stay calm in the process. I told her where Tommy had found the brooch, Mr. Oppenheim's evaluation of its age and worth, and Mr. Humphries' revelations about the one-time inhabitants of Penn Road. I even made a feeble attempt to explain the feeling I had when I held the brooch in my hands, the almost immediate obsession to find its owner, and return it to them. I tries to explain the haunting feeling that tragedy had hidden the brooch in the old fireplace, and the feeling that someone, somewhere, on this earth could tell me the secret.

Mary sat silently and sipped at her coffee while I verbally rushed through the last four days. It was impossible to read in her face what her thoughts were. Her expression changed only slightly from time-to-time as I talked. Some of the anxiety had gone out of her face by the time I finished, but it was evident that she did not feel the strong pull of the brooch I felt. She was, I believe, at the very least sympathetic to my fascination with an unknown event that had come to light so many years after the fact. What she was going to say eluded me, although I desperately searched her face for some clue.

She rose from the table and moved across the kitchen to pour herself another cup of coffee and get one for me. When she sat back down, she turned the brooch over in her hand, just as Mr. Oppenheim had done, studying the lady's face, and the initials on the back. She moved her mouth to say 'R.L.G.' but did not make a sound. Finally, she looked across her coffee cup to speak.

"Ninety years is a long time; we may have a tough time finding the owner."

She had said 'we,' signaling her approval! Yet, there was still not a hint of the obsession that I felt, while she had indirectly agreed to participate. Mary broke my train of thought when she spoke again.

"I wonder why in all that time they never came back for it?"

I suppose that question had been somewhere in the back of my mind as well. So many things could have transpired in that length of time. The person obviously could have died, moved, or been in prison for that matter. Anything could have occurred in such a long period of time.

"I know someone who has one almost exactly like it."

I asked, "Who?" My heart leaped up in my throat.

"Linda," she said.

"Linda, your sister? Where did she get it?"

Mary responded, "From mother, she gave Linda the cameo, and me the earrings that went with it before she died. They were one of her most prized possessions."

The earrings that go with it! My mind raced back to the conversation with Mr. Oppenheim and his telling about the matching earrings, and my throat was tight from the excitement.

"Mother said her mother had given them to her. She was very proud of them; there were only one or two others like them in town." I was straining to remember the earrings as Mary continued to talk. "Of course, I have never worn the earrings, one of the clasps was weak when Mother gave them to me, and it soon broke off in my jewelry box. I have meant several times over the years to see if I could have it fixed, but just never have. They are really very pretty earrings."

My mind was racing! I was trying to think if Mary's mother had

33

lived here all her life. I was trying to focus on 'a few in town.' Was that this town, Oakman? Was Mary's mother speaking of one of the owners of this brooch hidden in the chimney for so long? I was sure she had lived here all her life, but I had to ask to reassure myself. "Did your mother live here all her life?"

"They moved here when she was three years old. Why?"

"Well," I said, "if there were only a few in town, this one…" I held the brooch up in the air, "this one must have been one of them."

"Probably," Mary said in a matter-of-fact tone, "but she never said who owned the others, and she won't be able to tell us anything now." Mary's mother had been dead about eight years. Perhaps she had helped inadvertently. Just to know there were only a few, in my mind, seemed to narrow the field. Knowing that Linda had one and I had the other, for some reason, gave me a sense of relief I had not felt since I first held the brooch in my hand. I knew I had to do some calculations to discover whether the time periods matched one another, but in the back of my mind, I believed they did.

Mary's mother had no doubt known the owner of the cameo in my possession or at least, passed her on the street. If only Mary's mother were alive! She might know the fate of the unknown woman I was so desperately seeking. Of course, even if the fate of this woman was known to my decreased mother-in-law, she could not have known the fate of the brooch and gloves. Only the person who hid them there in a chimney on Penn Road could know. Until Tommy had freed them from the past, they had been hidden away.

Mary left to go and pick up the girls at someone's house and I was so involved with adding and subtracting time periods in my head that I was not really sure where she had said she was going.

Mr. Humphries said he was eighty-four years old; that would have meant he was born in 1904. Mary is forty-six years old, and she was born when her mother was forty-two years old. I had often jokingly blamed any trouble Mary had on being a 'mid-life crisis baby.' Her mother died eight years ago when Mary was thirty-eight. I calculated:

    46 (Mary's present age)
  +42 (Mary's mother's age at her birth)
  = 86.

That would mean that Mary's mother was born in 1900. I was very disappointed with the result of my computations. Ultimately, this meant that Mary's mother and Mr. Humphries probably knew one another, and both were too young to remember what had happened on Penn Road. Mary's mother, even if she were still alive, would have been, at the most, four years old, considering Mr. Humphries had said there was nothing there in his lifetime.

It finally occurred to me Mary's mother was talking about a different time than the one I needed to know about. A different set of people, younger than the lady who owned this brooch. Another dead end. It would have been Mary's grandmother who knew this lady, if indeed anyone did. It would be a generation before possessing firsthand knowledge of the residents of Penn Road and their fate.

The most I knew was that I had to begin to look at least eighty-four years ago for an answer, around the turn of the century, or even further back. I needed to take a break from this whole thing for a while, for my sanity and Mary's. Maybe hold off for a while, think it through, and take a more prepared approach. I did not really know where to look next, but I wanted to head off disappointment if I could. Perhaps the newspaper next, if it existed in 1900.

No matter what I did next, I had to quit shooting in the dark.

8

MARY PUT THE BROOCH IN A SMALL JEWELRY BOX, the kind a single piece would come in. It was about two inches by two inches and one inch deep, made of cardboard and covered with red velveteen, and hinged at one end so it could be opened. She placed it and the gloves in a plastic bag in her top dresser drawer, the one where you keep the things you only need to look at once a year or so; birth certificates, insurance papers, old letters and cards saved because they represented some special event. There were even a few of the children's school papers that represented some particular event that was above-and-beyond the average school day. She placed the brooch out of sight hoping we could move on without my having to constantly hold it in my hand or have it in my possession.

It was Mary who brought me to my senses and headed me in the right direction. She rationalized that what or whoever had lived there on Penn Road was there before the brooch. She believed, and convinced me, that I had all the information I was going to get about the brooch for the time being. What I really needed to know was whose house it was in which the brooch was hidden in the fireplace. Armed with that information, I might have a remote chance of connecting the two. She was right of course. Her grasp of the reality of the situation was much better than was mine. I hoped that the combination of the two would lead us in the right direction. Mary was participating in this inquiry into the past with a much calmer approach, and for that, I was thankful. My haphazard, passionate, and yet feeble approach had gotten me very little usable information. Mary's direction in the search would no doubt be more fruitful.

Mary's first endeavor was to take a spiral notebook, the kind the kids had always used in school, and begin a journal. I sat down at the kitchen table and began with Tommy bringing me the brooch.

March 25, 1988 (Friday): Tommy Morrow brought me a brooch found hidden in a fireplace, the last remaining structure on Penn Road.

March 26, 1988 (Saturday): Went to Oppenheim Jewelry, Springhill, and had brooch evaluated. Produced between 1850 to 1855 in Idar-Oberstein, Germany. Stone – brown and white mixture called Sardonyx. Earrings and necklace were originally sold with the brooch.

March 28, 1988 (Monday): Talked with Mr. Percy Humphries, old-time resident of Oakman. He informed me that Penn Road was at one time the Black section of town prior to 1904.

I noted, at this time, Tommy Morrow, Mr. Oppenheim, Mary, and I are the only ones to have seen the brooch. Only Tommy, Mary, and I know where it was found. The journal would consist of highlights of each piece of information. Just some notes to look back on so we would not be backtracking. I do not know precisely why it was essential to keep up with who knew about the existence of the brooch, but in the back of my mind, something told me I needed to know. I also had the feeling that Penn Road was going to be hard to get information on. Mr. Humphries knew nothing about it, and one would think that sometime, in his long life in Oakman, somebody would have said what happened there on Penn Road. Unless they did not want anyone to know.

Two weeks passed before I made another entry in the journal. Those two weeks were spent making a few phone calls, most of which, did not pan out. The *Oakman Sentinel* had not begun print until 1917. I went to the library and looked through the microfilm of the old papers. It seemed that it was several years following 1917 before the paper really began to print any news. For the first several years of its existence, it was more of a farmers' report than a newspaper; listing cotton prices, giving weather prediction, advertising the latest farm equipment, etc. Occasionally, there would be a story about a bumper crop or a pair of plow mules that could plow more land than any other pair in a single day. The paper seemed to steer clear of any real news. Of course, at the time I guess this was news to most of the people of Oakman.

It was at the county courthouse that a new mystery arose. I took my lunch break and went to inquire about old city land records or maps. The clerk at the courthouse was friendly but seemed to be perplexed to have to pull out old records in addition to all her many other duties. We rode the elevator to the basement of the new courthouse and she had me sign a ledger before I could enter the wire-walled file room. The room was sectioned off in the corner of the basement, having two concrete block walls on the back side, and two wire walls at the front. It was through a wire door that we entered this morgue of 'records past' that no one really needed. The clerk informed me that records twenty years back are kept on a computer, and anything else would be here.

"Now," she asked, "what exactly is it you want to know?"

I answered by stating, "I'd like to see a map of the city in or before 1904."

She studied the shelves and then moved to a bookcase that held perhaps two dozen huge, leather-bound books. She ran her finger across the row and when she found what she wanted, she pulled it out slightly and motioned me over to get it. The book was almost two feet tall, eighteen to twenty inches side to side, and three inches thick. The year '1900' was embossed on the binder. On the front it read:

Oakman, Alabama
Wayne County
1900
City and County
Maps

This was about as direct and to the point as it could have possibly been. I laid the large book on the table in the middle of the room and noticed a phone with no mechanism for dialing. The clerk was moving toward the wire door of the cage and talking before I could ask what the phone was for.

"When you finish," she informed me, "just pick up the phone and the operator will answer. Tell her you are in the basement records room and need to get out. She will call me." She had already moved out of the cage and was locking the wire door behind her. For a moment, I thought I would protest, but after all, I am sure this was standard procedure. I opened the large, dusty book and began to turn its pages when the clerk reappeared at the wire door and said, "take down whatever other books you need from the shelves, but leave anything you use on the table; it will have to be checked before it's returned to the shelves." She turned, and I heard the elevator close and ascend toward the upper floors.

In the first few pages were hand-drawn maps showing the city in its entirety. Buildings were sketched in on a small scale, but were made large enough to write in their significance; U.S. Post Office, Wayne Co, C.H., which I took to be the courthouse, county jail, etc. Streets were marked also. Then there were lines drawn vertically and horizontally across the pages. Each had an inscription penciled in somewhere in that area. Section 30, which I presumed from what I could figure out, dealt with the county. Township 10 indicted sections within the city limits as they existed at the time. I realized as I turned through the next pages that all information pertained to Township 10, which was Oakman. It was the section number that indicated a particular place. Oakman was, and is, the county seat for Wayne County. Township refers to a county seat and all areas surrounding it up to the boundary lines of that county.

I looked up Penn Road on the city map in the first few pages. Even in 1900, it ran along the railroad tracks. It was at that time in Township 10, Section 14. I could hardly believe the simplicity of these records. I imagined having to come back at least a half dozen times to locate Penn Road. I turned through the pages beyond the city map and located the two pages that were Section 14. There was no indication of any structures here, except the railroad tracks, but penciled in was all the information I needed, plus a passage I did not understand.

> *"From the northeast quarter of the northwest quarter of Section 14, Township 10 in range 7 contains 23 acres more or less. At this time, this is a settlement of colored people. No census exists as to its exact populace; I would guess 250 or more. It is a section containing perhaps 50 to 75 structures know to the people of this township as Pennsylvania. This section and its people are under their 35th year of government protection."* The entry was written right in the middle of this section and was signed, 'Thomas A. Stanley.

I looked across the room at the remaining books on the shelf and tried to ascertain if I had any idea what that last passage meant: "35th year of government protection." I returned to the shelf and one-by-one removed each book for the following years. The passages remained the same except that the year would change, 36th, 37th, and an estimation of the populace, perhaps 275, or more, etc. It was on the 1909 map that the passage abruptly changed.

> *"The northeast quarter of the northwest quarter of Section 14, Township 10, Range 7, 23 acres more or less, acquired by the city of Oakman in September of 1905."*

There was no mention of the houses or the people, no guess as to their populace. Just a description of the 23 acres and the fact that the city of Oakman had 'acquired' it. Up until 1905, Thomas A. Stanley had signed the various entries on these city maps and was named the head surveyor at the front of each book. In 1905, William A. Bell was listed as the head surveyor and signed the entries accordingly. The other notable change in the map was Penn Road. Up until this time, it ran the length of the 23 acres and extended on to the river, in my best estimation, a mile and a half or so. On the

1905 map, the road was shown to just end at the northern boundary of this 23 acres. Right in the middle of what had been the road was a note that read: 'D. Jackson Cotton Gin''. I knew right where that cotton gin and the warehouse that went with it were. Most of it was long ago torn down. Some of the original warehouse building is still there and is part of Jackson Lumber Company. There were further indications on the 1905 map of proposed construction along that mile and a half strip to the river that had been Penn Road:

"Proposed site: Powell Feed and Seed, W.B.,
Proposed site: Powell Foundry, W.B."

Mr. Bell had apparently decided a proposal to build only warranted his initials. I took my finger and followed what had been Penn Road toward the river. To my amazement, just about halfway was a note that read:

"Humphries' Dry Goods, presently under construction, W.B."

Like the others, it was being built in the middle of Penn Road. The sign on Mr. Humphries store door must have indicated 1905 or 1906. Only about forty-five minutes had passed while I was behind the locked door of the record room. I was glad that so much information had come so easily, but simultaneously was frustrated with the knowledge that I was still a long way from knowing what had happened to the settlement known as Pennsylvania after 1905. Accompanying this newly discovered knowledge was the question asking, 'why, right in the middle of the Heart of Dixie, not two miles from the Tennessee River, was there a settlement known as Pennsylvania?' I would have asked this question long before now had I been aware of what Penn Road was the abbreviation for. I had believed all my life, up until now it was named after someone of former prominence. I had never really given it much conscious thought. I assumed in my mind that this road was named after a Mr. Penn, whomever he might be.

I picked up the phone as I closed the map book and alerted the operator that I wished to be let out of the records room. She hesitated for a moment as if she might say, "Mrs. So-and-so has gone to lunch, you will have to wait." Instead she said, "Thank you," and hung up. It was a different clerk that appeared at the door with a key to let me out. She asked me to sign the register beside my name and she wrote: OUT – 12:05 p.m.

I was late, but only five minutes, maybe fifteen, by the time I was back at my desk. I spent the rest of the day feeling drained. My mind wandered as I pieced together what happened to Pennsylvania in 1905. When I arrived home that evening, I transferred my barely legible notes to the journal, completely filling the first page. Mary came in and sat down at the table and asked if the courthouse had provided any answers. I mumbled, "No, just a lot more questions," as I begin my entry into the journal:

April 11, 1988 (Monday): 1905 Pennsylvania disappeared from the map.

9

I'D ALMOST FORGOTTEN ABOUT TOMMY'S INVOLVEMENT in all this when he dropped by on Saturday morning. He said he had meant to stop by earlier, but his father was really working him hard. He said they were behind on several jobs. I asked how things were going out on Penn Road, and curiously he said things were not going at all. He told me the city had stopped the project indefinitely without explanation. Tommy said his father had gone down to the courthouse to raise hell. Mayor Bell told Jack the city had run into unexpected financial trouble and the library would just have to wait. Tommy continued saying that his father had really counted on that job, putting many things on hold because of it, and he was 'damn sure' going to find out what was going on.

Tommy did not ask me a thing about the brooch or anything I had discovered. I was glad in a way that he had not. Jack Morrow was already mad at the world; I cared nothing about having him mad at me. I did not want to give him a reason to think I was leading Tommy astray. He looked at his watch, said he was late, and drove away. When Tommy pulled into the driveway, I was on my way to review what I had garnered from the city maps. I did not know how it would help, but for the time being, I was at a standstill. Mary had written the State Historical Society asking for a referral to someone of authority on the history of this part of the state. We were waiting for a reply.

I headed out for the day and drove to what I now knew to be the remains of Pennsylvania. I walked out into the open field and looked in all directions. To the south, the most noticeable thing was a very tall radio antenna. The east offered nothing but the back of a row of houses. To the west on a slight incline was Brewer Elementary

School. It was the oldest in the city, and it looked ancient. There was more of a look of an old plantation house about the building than appearing as a school. It was two stories high with four large columns holding up part of the roof and a balcony that looked out over the railroad tracks and beyond even Pennsylvania. It had been bricked at one time or another. I had only a vague recollection of when that was done or what it looked like before. To the north, which was the direction Penn Road used to go, was Jackson Lumber Company. Beyond it, I could see nothing since the lumber company buildings blocked the view.

I returned to the car and drove up Main Street which ran parallel with what was Penn Road toward the river. I tried to drive slowly and look as much as possible at something I had been looking at all of my life, but now with a different perspective. Penn Road would have been to my left as I drove. First thing was downtown Oakman, a part of town that tried desperately to survive what progress had done. With the construction of shopping centers and the movement of town away from this area came its virtual death. Only about every third or fourth storefront had a business within, and they appeared to have no customers. A few businesses like Humphries' had survived, but even their customers were few.

As I left the old downtown area, with Penn Road still to the left, there was a much busier section: the new Wayne County Courthouse, the County Jail, the Post Office, Health Department, etc., all newly constructed or remodeled in the last fifteen or twenty years. From here to the river were office complexes full of lawyers, doctors, accountants, and any other professionals one might need, as well as some remaining homes and some Civil War historical markers. The end of Main Street crossed the Interstate leading west out of town. Once you crossed the Interstate coming into town, you were in what has, for all my life and Mr. Humphries' been called the Black section of town. This section ran along the river in both directions east and west. It was a picture of deprivation and sorrow that surely no man wishes still existed. Houses with Black children playing in yards with no grass, roofs bowing down that could not possibly shed water, broken windows, and torn screen doors. It looked, I could imagine, very much as Pennsylvania looked ninety years ago.

I drove for a time occasionally waving at people on their front porches or standing in the street, and thought I might roll down my window to ask an older resident about Pennsylvania, but then how could I possibly explain myself, let alone such a question?

It was when I started back out to cross the Interstate that I saw something I had never seen in my life or at least never taken notice of. Down by the river, overlooking its banks, was a small cemetery and church. The land descended toward the river and was so low that they were barely visible from the street.

I turned and drove right up to the fence. I got out of the car to get a better look. The cemetery overlooked the river and had it not been for a tree line that grew along the bank it would have possessed a beautiful view. Around the circumference of the cemetery was a low white picket fence in need of repair. The white pointed slats were peeling and cracked; some swayed in the wind while others had completely given up and fallen to the ground.

The tiny gate that entered the cemetery leaned to one side and was secured by a rusty hinge and a length of rotten rope. I leaned against the fence, being careful not to push any more of it down and strained to look at the decaying headstones marking each of the graves. Many were worn and broken, leaning in all directions, some sinking into the ground. Many, if not most, were not even headstones in the traditional sense. Just a rock with a now unreadable name carved on its face. A tiny cedar cross looked as if it would melt in a hard rain, and from my vantage point, none were legible enough to read. Then, right in the middle of this miserable, forgotten place was a huge oak tree that appeared to be the axis around which all the graves revolved. It was six feet or larger in diameter with long high and low limbs that, if it were alive, would appear to shade the entire cemetery. The roots at the base protruded like giant arms that sustained it from the wind. It looked as if time had hardened it to stone like the grave markers its limbs reached out to cover. It had died, it appeared, with the ground and graves it protected. As I stood there, engrossed in the sorrow of this place, I heard a voice in the distance to my left. It was coming from the church. I, for the moment, had forgotten the church was even there. I turned after the voice had called to me, I thought perhaps several times. Standing on the steps of the church was a large Black man in grey pants and a white shirt. I had to stop and take my mind away from the tree to understand what he said.

"Can I help you with something sir?" He repeated the question several times before I moved toward him. He smiled as I came closer, extended his hand for me to shake, and asked once more, "Can I help you, sir?"

I reached out and took his hand, apologizing for not answering when he called.

He looked out toward the cemetery. "No apology necessary, brother, won't you come in out of the sun?" He motioned toward the front door of the church and introduced himself as we went in, "I'm Revered Nathan Young. What might be your name, sir?"

"Bob Wallace," I replied, as I began to survey the inside of the church. The pews were rough and homemade. The wooden floor had been painted and repainted until three or four different colors showed through. Several of the windows were broken and had been repaired with cardboard and tape. The interior walls were boards that ran in horizontal lines from front to back and had separated from each other with time. The wind from the river whistled through the walls and windows in a very faint whisper. At the front of the church were a single pulpit and a cane-bottom chair for the minister. On the wall behind the altar, one cross made of wood hung from the ceiling. I was still looking at the cross when Reverend Young spoke again.

"Were you looking for something in particular or just looking?"

I replied, "to be honest, I have lived in Oakman most of my life and never knew this cemetery was here. I just happened across it and stopped to look. Does it have a name?"

Reverend Young replied, "This is Lazarus Cemetery, and that oak tree that took your senses away is the Lazarus Tree."

"Lazarus…" I had not asked a question, but Revered Young

anticipated I would.

He said, "This cemetery was a slave cemetery before the Civil War. A plantation owner by the name of Brewer set it aside for his slaves to bury their dead. After the war, free Black men came here and built this church and continued to bury their dead in the cemetery. The story, as I understand it, is that the first person to preach over a burial here eulogized the deceased by using the story of Jesus raising Lazarus from the dead. The preacher stood under that oak tree as he preached, so the people began to call it Lazarus Cemetery and the Lazarus Tree."

I was embarrassed to ask if the church was still used for services, but I asked him anyway. Reverend Young replied, "Oh, no. The congregation built a new church up the street thirty years ago or more. That was long before my time. I come here once a month, open the door and windows to air it out, and make sure the roof isn't leaking."

My next question might be the one he could not answer. "Do you know how many people are buried in the cemetery?" I was afraid accompanying that question he might want to know why I wanted to know or cared, but he didn't.

He took it in stride and seemed eager to provide an answer stating, "Well, come with me, and we will see." Revered Young continued, "the original register of burials is kept at the new church."

We walked up the street four blocks to a newer brick building perhaps four times the size of the old one there on the river. We went in the back door and down a hallway to Reverend Young's office where he offered me a seat in front of his desk as he moved to open the bottom drawer of a locked filing cabinet. He took out an old leather book with a string wrapped around it. He sat down at his desk, slipped the string over the book, and opened it stating, "Now, this ledger was not actually started until after the end of the Civil War, but one of the past ministers of the church took it upon himself to investigate the previous burials. I believe this to be as accurate an account as possible of the history of the Lazarus Cemetery." He continued, with the air of someone teaching a class, "this last burial was in September of 1917. At that time there were known to be 153 people buried in Lazarus Cemetery."

He pushed the register across the desk and I instinctively began to look for the year 1905. There were sixteen people buried in the cemetery that year. Eleven of them were buried on the same day, according to the register, July 5, 1905. Their names, according to the listing, were those of seven men, two women, and apparently, two bodies that could not be identified, listed in the register just as 'mother and infant child.' I showed the listing to the Reverend Young and asked if he had ever heard an explanation for that many deaths at one time. He had not, but suggested, considering the period of time, no doubt an epidemic of some type had claimed their lives, typhoid or yellow fever perhaps. He had given all the information he had. Reverend Young walked me back to the Lazarus Cemetery, shook my hand, and invited me to come back at any time. I graciously thanked him and started back to my car, taking another lingering look toward the Lazarus Tree.

It was not until I turned the car around and headed south that I looked up and realized I spent the morning unaware of where I had come from. As I left the cemetery I stopped the car short of the street and got out to see if what I thought I had seen was real. The radio antenna I had seen at the south end of Pennsylvania rose above every building in its path. Looking over my shoulders at the Lazarus Tree behind me to North and then back again toward the antenna in the South, I realized that I had come to the destination I was looking for. I could see clearly that Penn Road had come to this exact location before buildings were built across it, Pennsylvania Road had led directly to the Lazarus Tree!

I was quickly becoming aware of how oblivious a person can be to what has come and gone around him. I was not quite sure what it was that I really knew, but I knew there was a secret hidden in Oakman. A secret that at least two generations had spent almost a hundred years trying to cover up. I was utterly absorbed in the knowledge that I held the key to a secret that probably most of the people who had tried to hide Pennsylvania Road did not even know.

I had in my possession the only two things left on earth that could lead to the to the road that was intentionally conceled–a ladie's brooch and gloves.

I filled the journal with everything I had discovered on April 16, 1988. While I recorded the information I had discovered at Lazarus Cemetery, I realized that most likely I was the only one who could understand what I had written because it merely suggested that there was something hidden in the past; at this point, I made no attempt to try and explain what it was.

10

IT WAS THE END OF APRIL BEFORE MARY FOUND THE
person we needed and who had been right under our noses all along.
Mary had written the State Historical Society; they, in turn, referred
her to the Wayne County Society, which led her to Mrs. Laura Belle
Davis. Mrs. Davis, we were soon to learn, was president, or past
president, of everything that had gone on in Oakman in the past
thirty or more years. She was also a lifetime member of both the
Daughters of the American Revolution and the Daughters of the
Confederacy. I gathered from reading the letter from the county
society that she was bathed in a great deal of Oakman's past.

I called Mrs. Davis and made an appointment to see her. She
appeared, from all indications to be thrilled that at least one person
beside herself wanted to know about the past. She asked that I come
by her house on Monday, May 2, at 5:00 p.m., and as she gave me
directions, I realized that I knew precisely where it was. I had passed
it perhaps a hundreds of times in my lifetime, but I had never known
who lived there.

I was eager to get to Mrs. Davis's house on Monday and spent
most of the afternoon at my desk trying to pass the time as hurriedly
as I possibly could. I still felt the obsession bubbling up inside of me
that I had felt at the beginning of my quest. I was trying very hard to
control that obsession so it would not consume me as it had before.
I arrived in front of Mrs. Davis's house about ten minutes early. I sat
in the car and looked at her house, a large, gothic structure, probably
one of a kind, two and one-half stories high with a porch that
wrapped around on three sides the best I could tell. On the two front
corners were round rooms that extended through two floors capped

off with a pointed cone-shaped roof. As I stared, the house began to look like a castle. It was definitely the house of a historian, a person who very much wishes to hold on to her past.

I went to the front porch and pulled the chain of the bell to the right of the door facing. It was a very long elaborate brass form. The shape of an angel secured it to the wall with wings spreading fully out in the opposite directions. The angels' hands were thrust forward holding a staff on which the bell pivoted as I pulled down on the chain. As I did, the bell rang out in a musical tone that was as pleasant as a robin singing in the trees. The bell brought Mrs. Davis to the door immediately, and I was sure she was sitting, waiting for it to sound. She opened the door and said, "Mr. Wallace?" as if to clarify before she opened the door all the way back.

"Yes ma'am," I stated.

Mrs. Davis opened the door fully as she introduced herself. "I'm Laura Davis. Won't you come in?"

She was not quite what I expected. Her age was hard to estimate, her hair and dress were immaculate, but her skin was wrinkled and her chin flaccid, as inevitably occurs with age. Her home was steeped in history, including paintings and furniture from the past everywhere I looked. She led me around a vast, elaborate staircase that ascended to the next floor into an old library that looked like a museum. Shelves full of old books, newspaper articles from the past framed and carefully hung on the walls, a spinning wheel standing guard in one corner, a gun cabinet full of old weaponry. Even a Confederate cap in a glass case lay atop a massive desk that stood guard over it all. It was not possible to take it all in as Mrs. Davis offered me a chair.

"Now then, how may I help you?" She spoke with a heavy aristocratic Southern drawl. Although my first impulse was to ask about the brooch, I thought for the time being, I would stay away from that subject. I was not ready to reveal it yet, if at all. So, I started with part of the truth.

"You see, Mrs. Davis, I am an amateur archaeologist of sorts, and recently I discovered that there must have at one time been a settlement on Penn Road at the railroad tracks, but I can find no exact record of its existence."

She looked at me with the same friendliness as before, but more questioning. She knew just what I was thinking about and she was going to answer. She sighed as she began to talk. "That is a question I've never been asked. You see, people older than I would not talk about it, and people younger than I had no knowledge of it. That settlement on Penn Road was before the Civil War the slave quarters for a landowner named Daniel Brewer. He owned a great deal of what is now known as Wayne County. Part of the original house became what is now Brewer Elementary School. Mr. Brewer was a wealthy man who owned thousands of acres of land, but he was known to be a different kind of slave owner than most. You see, he had inherited his power, money, and land from his father. Daniel truly did not believe in slavery, but he also had more foresight at the time than perhaps the federal government. He knew that simply setting his slaves free with nowhere to go was not the answer. Daniel felt that keeping them and treating them fair was a better solution. So, he did just that, paying them for their work, allowing them to sharecrop his land, and so forth. Although he felt he was doing the right thing, his reputation and power in the South were rapidly declining because of it. Articles appeared in the papers of that time accusing him of having a Black woman for a mistress as well as children with her. As the war approached, he was labeled a traitor and a Yankee sympathizer; several attempts were made on his life. There was even talk of the state about taking his land and exiling him from the South, but then the war came, and, for a time, he was left insulated from it. During the war, he simply voiced no opinion one way or the other. He did not believe in the South's cause, but he would not take up arms against his birthright."

Mrs. Davis appeared to have wanted to tell this story for some time, but the opportunity had never presented itself. She continued, "Just as the war was coming to an end, Daniel Brewer, was found shot to death in his bed. No one was arrested for the crime. For a time, his slaves, almost all of which had remained with him

52

throughout the war, were at the mercy of an angry and beaten South. Some of them were hanged by lynch mobs using his murder as an excuse. The men were put in shackles and moved from place to place to dig trenches for the Confederacy as it turned to fight one more time. The women were left here in Oakman to be brutalized and assaulted. It was not for several months after Lee's surrender that Union troops arrived in force and freed those unfortunate souls from their bondage. It was then that the people of Oakman learned that Daniel Brewer had reached out from his grave to help his slaves be free. When Federal troops arrived, they carried with them news that would shock the entire South."

Mrs. Davis stopped there and said I would have to excuse her for a moment. She left the room and returned shortly with coffee on a wooden tray. She didn't ask if I wanted any, she just poured me a cup, sat down, and went on with her story.

"You see, Mr. Brewer had done two things: one, he deeded to his slaves two parcels of land. One was the twenty or so acres along Penn Road, which is where they lived, and the other was four hundred acres along the river in the area where he had given them land for a cemetery, the cemetery known as Lazarus Cemetery. It was discovered that the rest of the holdings left to him by his father had been sold off little by little long before the war except for a few small parcels which he left to the city, one of which is where the school stands now. He also arranged with his powers to offer these now-freed slaves Federal protection for a period to span forty years after the war's end. Now that passage on the city map made sense, "in their thirty-fifth year of Federal protection."

Mrs. Davis continued with her story but was breathing more heavily now, and I believed the story was coming to an end.

"Daniel Brewer, I think, believed he was doing the right thing, but you see, without seed and tools to farm the land he had left them, they continued to be at the mercy of outraged, defeated people. Many people had come out of the war with less than the people they were fighting to enslave. So the land on the river, other than the church and cemetery, remained, for the most part, idle up until the turn of the century, when the Black people, who had grown in number, moved to and settled on what was intended to be farmland. Their plight was essentially the same as any other Blacks who remained in the South after the war, except they were landowners. However, land they could not use."

I let her breathe a minute before I asked any questions. She appeared tired from her long speech but glad that she had a chance to pass the story along.

"Mrs. Davis," I began, "do you know what happened to the houses there in Pennsylvania?"

She answered, "They were burned in a fire that accidentally started in someone's fireplace, I believe. 1905, I think. The people moved, began again there on the river, and as far as I know, the city eventually bought or took the land for back taxes."

I asked, "Do you know why they called the settlement Pennsylvania?"

She was exhausted now, I could tell by her breathing, somehow she looked older and frailer than she did at the door. She looked up at a painting over the fireplace of a man with a dark beard. She looked as if she might ask him if he had anything to add.

"That man was my husband." She pointed over the fireplace with her eyes. "He was a true historian. If he were still alive, he might be able tell you."

"I tried to find this information in the paper, but the *Sentinel...*" She stopped me short before I could say anything else.

"Oh, no, you were looking in the wrong newspaper. You need to look at the *Sommerville War and Peace.*"

Sommerville was a spot on the road ten miles from town that could be easily missed. I had no idea it had ever been large enough to support a newspaper.

She continued, "Sommerville was the county seat up until 1915. It was a much larger and more progressive town before and after the Civil War. There was, at one time, two cotton gins, a foundry, and a sawmill there. Once they built the bridge across the river, there was just no reason to come or go out that way anymore, so in time, the town for the most part up and died. But they had a newspaper before the Civil War, and it survived right up until the town died. That is the paper you want to read."

"Where are those papers now? Surely there is no library there."

"No library," she answered, "but strangely enough, they keep the newspapers carefully preserved in the vault at the one remaining city building. The courthouse, which was at one time the center of our county seat. If you like, I can arrange for you to see them. I have tried for years to have these papers moved here to Oakman or to the University, but I have not been successful. Those newspapers are really about all that is left of their pride in Sommerville."

I questioned, "What do I need to do see them?"

She was writing on a slip of paper and handed it to me as she talked, "You call me whenever you can take a day to go out there and I will arrange it for you. You will need the whole day if not more."

I was elated. This was what I had been looking for all along, a firsthand look into the past. Mrs. Davis walked to the front door and showed me out, as with the Reverend Young, inviting me back at any time.

Mrs. Davis told me to be sure and call her any time stating, "I may even go out there with you to Sommerville if you do not mind. I do not drive anymore, and I love to go out there myself."

Of course, I thanked her and told her I would be honored to have such an authority as her to accompany me to Sommerville. I climbed back in my car feeling drained. Now that I had half of the story I wanted, perhaps the *Sommerville War and Peace* would provide me with some insight into the rest.

May 2, 1988: Met with Mrs. L. Davis – she told me everything…

Mrs. Laura Davis's revelations were more than I had hoped for, but there was something or someone still missing. There was another story there at the Lazarus Cemetery. There was a reason for this migration to the river and the town cutting these people off by building across their path back to Pennsylvania. The townspeople had in effect built a blockade to keep the residents of Pennsylvania from returning to their homeplace. Granted, by Mrs. Davis's account, there were no homes to return to, but Pennsylvania had been their home. This piece of earth had been their refuge from the world for perhaps a hundred years or more. Generation upon generation had been born on this land. Daniel Brewer had tried to give them sanctuary from the people they feared. Why would they leave and build houses on the farmland that was the only hope of survival for the children not yet born?

Obliterating Penn Road would not in itself have kept them from returning. It was the implied barrier, very effective at that time. Covering Penn Road with new construction in effect drew the boundary between White and Black. Obviously, intentional, they had pushed the Black population as far away from the White as they could without pushing them into the river and perhaps at one time that had been considered. To push them into the river and drown them and remove them from sight and mind. Mrs. Davis had said they simply went there, rebuilt, and settled again. I knew in my heart there was more to it than that. There was still the brooch and the gloves, still that secret to deal with. What part it and the woman who owned the items had played in the destruction of Pennsylvania was still to be known. Mrs. Davis knew of only an accidental fire that destroyed an entire community. If she had any knowledge other than that, she had not revealed it to me.

I drove back to Lazarus Cemetery on Wednesday following my meeting with Mrs. Davis. I tried again to strain across the fence and look at the names on the decaying headstones, still with no luck. The markers were too old, too worn. Time had taken its toll. I turned to look again at the radio tower in the distance and tried to imagine what the road had looked like before it was covered by the relentless march of time and progress. I knew I needed to go inside the fence to get a closer look at the forgotten graves the frail and broken fence tried so despairingly to secure.

I wanted to touch the Lazarus Tree in hopes that it might reveal some part of this mystery to me. It had stood there for longer than any of the forgotten lives its limbs spread out to shelter. It had, no doubt, wept with mourners that had come here so long ago to bury and grieve for their dead. I felt that somewhere there under the protection of its massive and sheltering limbs was at the very least a part of the answer I was seeking.

I needed to talk with Reverend Young once again. I needed to obtain permission to go inside the fence and look at what was left of a time I so desperately wanted to know more about. It was late now, I would wait until I could come early and have has as much light as I could possibly get.

11

SPRING HAD ARRIVED QUICKLY; I BARELY REMEMBER the trees turning green. The Lazarus Tree remained the lifeless, faded grey it had been for years. It was hard to imagine that it had ever been green and alive, but it must have been to reach the massive proportions it was now. Even in death it seemed to stand its post without wavering. When the wind came in across the river and scattered the dust from the interstate and blew the other trees along the river back and forth, the Lazarus Tree remained steady and calm. Its branches stretched out in every direction and refused to bend or to bow to the wind. The smallest of its limbs on the very end of its massive reach would only quiver slightly as the wind passed through them, but even the frailest of limbs never seemed to succumb to the force of the wind. They remained, for the most part, intact as did the rest of the tree.

I had come back to the Lazarus Cemetery on Saturday morning, May 7th, after I could not reach Mrs. Davis. I called Reverend Young and asked if I might go inside the fence and walk through the graves to see if they held any further information that might point me in the direction I needed to go. I quite frankly had no idea whatsoever what direction to pursue. I tried Mrs. Davis several times on the phone to arrange to go to Sommerville, but so far had no luck in contacting her. The Reverend Young was just as he had been before. He was friendly and unquestioning. He told me he would meet me at the cemetery at eight thirty on Saturday morning and would assist me in any way he could. He explained that he had no objection to my going into the cemetery alone, but since passers-by might question my presence there, it would perhaps be better if he were with me to explain.

I wondered as I hung up the phone what he might say to anyone that asked. After all, I had not given him an explanation for my inquiries. I thought of several ideas he might have about my curiosity; perhaps he thought I just discovered there was a Black ancestor somewhere in my family tree or a grandchild's dark complexion I could not explain. No matter, he had not asked and, to be honest, I was not at all sure how I would answer if he did. I had arrived early, about seven thirty, although not at all intentionally. It was just that my lack of patience had overcome me. I had walked the length and width of the cemetery outside the fence and observed the Lazarus Tree from every direction. I stopped and strained across the fence as I made my way around I, trying to see the name or date on a headstone. As before, when I had only stood near the gate, a complete notation was impossible to see. I could make out a number or letter occasionally, but never a complete date or name. As I made my way around the fence, I wondered if going inside would help. The markers appeared to be so worn with time I was beginning to believe that even an up-close view might not reveal any more than I could see from outside the fence.

I could see clearly that many of the headstones were broken and therefore incomplete. At best, any information I would obtain would be only partial, unless there was something I could not see from the fence. Perhaps something complete and left intact even though time had so obviously taken its toll on most of the memorials to mark the dead. It was also a possibility that many of the markers, especially the earliest, had never been inscribed in the first place. They were only marked with a stone from the banks of the river so no one body would be buried over another. There were also those that had no doubt, never been marked at all, the graves of those few that had no family to see that some memory of their existence should be placed at the head of their graves. Perhaps, something someone always intended to do but never got it accomplished. Then there were always those like the grave in the record called 'mother and infant child,' those souls just passing through who nobody really knew their name.

As Reverend Young came up the sidewalk and around the corner of the church, he waved and turned to go inside. I waited patiently by the gate and could hear the sounds of windows sliding open. He had undoubtedly thought this to be an opportune time to let the church air out; that had been the reason he was there on my first visit. He came out of the door shortly with the same friendly smile on his face as before, waving and talking as he moved toward me. I glanced down to look at my watch, hoping he would not notice.

Precisely eight thirty, he was right on time. He greeted me by stating, "How do you do, Mr. Wallace? Good to see you again. Wonderful day, isn't it?"

I answered him stating, "Sorry to take up your time on a Saturday." Although I said it, I knew deep down I really didn't mean it. I wanted to go inside the fence, and if he had to come with me, I was glad it was today. He would, no doubt, be of help and I was glad he was here.

"No bother, I have intended myself to walk through this old cemetery for years," he answered. He reached around in the back pocket of his black baggy pants and brought out several sheets of folded, white paper stating, "I brought some copies here of the records. I thought they might help. I also found this map in the back of the old ledger. Seems to be a layout of the cemetery." He was unfolding the paperwork as he spoke, "Don't know who drew it, the author's name is not on it. Seems to be a lot newer than the ledger itself."

Reverend Young held out in both hands a piece of white paper about twice the size of the copied papers he had handed to me to hold. Across the top was printed in ink: *Lazarus Cemetery 1938*. The piece had been folded and refolded until some of the creases were torn. The tiny rectangles that covered it and lettering inside the rectangles were, for the most part, legible, except in a few places where the folds of the paper had come across them. I bent over and strained my eyes to read the small lettering confined to the rectangles, and in doing so, I could see most of them.

Well over half of the graves on the map were lettered *UNK* to represent that the grave occupants were 'unknown.' Some had only a first name, but no last name while others only had a year inscribed within the rectangle. Others had a first and last name along with the month, day, and year. Even the colossal oak had been crudely drawn in the middle of the paper. In a circle around the tree, the creators of the map had carefully inked in **The Lazarus Tree**. Just from taking a brief glance at the map it appeared that the oldest graves were just far enough out from the tree to be away from the roots that ran along the ground, maybe eight or ten feet. The cemetery then spread out from there in all directions. After a few rows of graves, there seemed to be no method of pattern to the dates. One was marked 1870, no name. On either side of it were two with 19 and 7 inked in. There was, I am quite sure, some reason for the pattern and arrangement of the graves, but it had long since been lost with most of the names of the people who lay below the ground.

After surveying the map for a few minutes, the Reverend folded it over and began to work on the old wooden gate that had not been opened for such a long time. He at first tried unsuccessfully to remove, intact, the rope that secured the gate, but quickly discovered that it was more dust than rope. Then he very carefully brought the gate back on its one remaining hinge and let the bottom rest on the ground. We both entered and stood for a moment just inside the gate looking back and forth over what now seemed more like ancient ruins than an abandoned cemetery. Almost immediately upon stepping inside the fence that had for so long guarded this place against the outside world, I began to see things I had not seen from the outside.

The Lazarus Tree was even more enormous than it had appeared. It was more gnarled and twisted than I thought. Throughout the grounds that lay within the fence, there were more than just the upright headstones I had seen before. Many of the graves had bricks that lay across their entire width and length. Some had stones stacked a foot high or higher in an oblong fashion, a pyramidal shape covering the entire area. Still, others were surrounded by the remains of a frail stone or wooden fences that sometimes enclosed one or more graves. As I looked out across the

61

width and length of the cemetery, I had a feeling that there were many cemeteries within the one; families who had carefully reserved enough ground for burying each member close to the other. Small children were carefully buried beside or at the feet of their mothers and father.

In every direction lay broken and falling markers, some with the detached pieces carefully leaned against the bottom of the headstone. Many of the pieces were nowhere in sight, no doubt tossed across the fence or covered with dirt from another grave. One directly in front of me, as I stood just inside the fence, had broken into many pieces. The pieces had then been stacked at the head of the grave so that they became the memorial to the person that lay beneath it.

After looking back and forth over the cemetery from inside the fence, Reverend Young and I moved in two different directions. He moved toward the west side of the cemetery; I moved directly toward the Lazarus Tree. I ambled along continuing to look up and down the tree as I moved. The upper limits of the tree were out of sight quickly because of its skyward reach. I got to the base of the tree and reached out to touch it, hoping I think, for something magical to happen. A dream or vision, anything that would help me see what I wanted to see. I felt myself being consumed once again, obsessed with the need to know. My hand sensed the tree but nothing more. The large trunk of the tree felt more like stone than wood, hard and lifeless. Even with the sun shining down, it was cold to the touch. The low-hanging limbs that I could see above my head were also massive, almost like trees in themselves.

Around the base of the tree was a ring of rusty nails, driven into the tree as if something had been attached to it at some time. Small pieces of decaying wood still clung under the heads of some of the square-headed nails. As I walked around the circumference of the tree, I could follow the nails around to each side excepting a short distance on the south side of the tree. Just on the south side, facing Pennsylvania, there was a void and there, on the ground, was a cement marker. Simply constructed, there was very little design to it. It was rounded slightly at the top, fifteen inches or so wide, protruding from the ground perhaps two feet. The marker, like so many of the others, had twisted and turned with time. It leaned back toward the Lazarus Tree and then sank into the ground slightly, causing the marker to lean to the left. I got down on my knees in front of the stone to see if the inscription on its face was still legible. The marker was crusted over with time. Sand and dirt, blow by the wind and moistened by the rain, had clung to the stone and hardened to its surface becoming almost a part of its makeup. In the face of the stone, although time had tried very hard to cover it, the letters were still visible. Crudely cut into the marker were the words: **Mother and Child**. Under the letters was the date **July 5, 1905.** Nothing more. The grave obviously stretched out away from the tree at a right angle, north to south, with the marker being carefully placed with its back against the tree at the north end of the grave. The earth that had once been used to cover it had sunk below ground level years ago and I felt that if not for a very few inches of dirt, I would see the top of a coffin.

Two of the large roots that grew along the ground from the tree twisted and turned nearly encircling the grave. I wondered for a moment why this place was chosen. Even eighty-some-odd years ago these huge roots would have been hard to contend with. Surely, even when this tree was eighty-three years younger, the roots that ran under the ground would have had to have been cut and chopped through to make a resting place for this mother and child. I found it strange, as I looked around in every direction that this was the only grave out of so many that was placed right against the tree. I also noticed at a glance, back and forth, that this appeared to be the only grave that was dug with its length running north to south rather than east to west like the others.

As I stood again, I almost walked back into the grave between the roots before catching myself and stepping sideways out of it. When I did regain an upright position to the side of the headstone, I found myself wondering if mother and child were buried in the same coffin since there appeared to be no distinction that there were two graves. My daydreaming ended with the Reverend Young calling me to the west end of the cemetery.

"Mr. Wallace, if you please."

His voice sounded much farther off than it could possibly have been, given the confines of the cemetery fence. The distance in his voice was more of time than space. I had not finished daydreaming when he called out to me. I was still feeling the same agony and pain that had come and gone out of the frail wooden gate that cut this ground and its people off from the world outside.

"Mr. Wallace, here is something that might be of interest to you."

This time his voice broke my concentration, and I moved away from the grave at the foot of the Lazarus Tree, although I felt it was holding on to me with a choking grasp. I pulled away and moved through the graves to the southwest corner of the cemetery where Reverend Young was waiting. He was looking down at a stone-covered lot at this corner of the cemetery that contained the graves of nine people who had died on the same day. All of the nine graves were covered with stones laid side-by-side that covered all of them collectively. In the middle of the stonework small stones had been broken up and placed in such a way as to show the date, July 5, 1905. Then, at the head of the stone-covered plot were nine individual stones with the names of those who died, crudely carved in the face of each. Nine in all, just as the old ledger had stated.

As with so many of the other markers, the individual monuments were worn and faded, covered with time. They, like the others, were very difficult to read. There were two women's stones which read, Laura Field and Beatrice Peo...? The rest of Beatrice's last name was no longer legible. The other stones were even more difficult to read upon close observation. Harry H..., one with only the letters J and G showing through the crust time had left. It was impossible to tell where the G even came in the name. The other five were like the rest: a part of a name, a letter or two, but nothing complete.

I unfolded the copies of the old ledger that Revered Young had handed me as we came in the gate of the cemetery. It was on second observation not as complete as I thought when I looked at it for the first time in his office. These graves were noted in the ledger, as was the date July 5, 1905, but the other information in the ledger was essentially the same as I could see in front of me. Broken letters, parts of names, but, like the stones, incomplete.

Reverend Young interrupted my thoughts again. "Probably died in an epidemic of some sort. Yellow fever, typhoid, something like that. Covered the whole place so the disease couldn't get out. That's what they believed back then…"

What they had died of was no longer on my mind or even their names. It was the date of July 5, 1905. The same day as the woman and child buried under the Lazarus Tree. The unexplained details were rushing through my mind at a pace I could hardly keep up with. Was it possible that the mother and child had died in a totally unrelated incident on the same day? If this mother and infant child had died of the same illness, why had they not been buried under the cover of the stone barrier just as were the others? Even if mother and child had not died of some terrible, contagious disease, as the Revered Young believed, why had the people who buried them gone back to where the cemetery began to bury them? Not only to where the cemetery began but even further, to a place where no one had ever been buried before, so close to the tree. One thought raced back and forth through my mind as I stood motionless, staring at the ledger but not reading it. At one time, these nine markers had borne the names of the people who lay beneath them. Why had there never been any attempt to name this mother and child? Their inscription was never meant to identify them by name, now or ever! Why?

The Reverend Young had moved away from me to another part of the cemetery. He had thought these particular graves would interest me. Apparently, they had not interested him as much. Of course, he had not seen, or perhaps not noted in the ledger, that the mother and child's grave bore the same date as his epidemic plot. I wondered, as my eyes moved away from the copies of the ledger back to the stones laid side by side on the ground if any of these graves belonged to children? If they did, there was no distinction between them and the others. The stones formed a rectangle along the ground that covered the nine graves completely. The stones that bore each one's name were of approximately the same width and height. If there were children buried under this tomb meant to keep the living safe from the deadly disease it was not detectable. That, in itself, was strange. Children, it seems were quite often the first to die when these incurable sicknesses ran rampant. My mother had lost a younger sister and brother to one of these diseases. I can recall my father telling of his twin brother's high fever that almost killed him. I remember my father saying my grandmother kept his brother on a blanket laid on the floor because it was cooler there and quite often my father said he had to go under the bed after his twin, where he had rolled in his confusion to try and escape the heat of the fever. From all outward indications, there were no children buried here.

I turned and walked away to survey the rest of the graves. There were none like these nine. There were husband and wives, beloved sons and daughter, small children, some buried alone, others near their parents. Some families were closed off from the rest of the cemetery by small stones or wooden fences, now toppled or decaying. Many of the graves had been covered with block or stone, but nowhere else in the cemetery were there nine distinct souls confined under one barrier. None of the markers I could read bore the same month, day, and year. Several had died the same year. I even recognized two from the same month and year, but nowhere were they buried like those that died on July 5, 1905.

Eventually, I worked my way back around to the Lazarus Tree. As I walked, I realized that Reverend Young was there, in the cemetery, but I only sensed his presence from time-to-time never acknowledging he was there to him or myself. I wondered if he had come by the Lazarus Tree while I was not paying attention. I wondered if he, too, had connected this grave marked mother and child to the other nine. As I stood at the foot of this sunken place in the ground, I wrestled with myself as to whether or not to include him in my thoughts. To do so, I would almost assuredly have to give him all the information I had: Pennsylvania, the fire, the brooch, everything! If not, there would be no way for him to understand my interest, even if all this information would help to clarify it in his mind. After all, he was Black, and this was a story of Black people, He could, no doubt, be of great help to me. I stared back up at the massive limbs of the tree, stepping back a few feet to see farther up the top. I walked around the base of the tree again, stepping over the roots that ran on top of the ground, looking at the nails twisted, bent and driven through the bark that still clung to the body of the tree. Reverend Young was upon me before I realized it and I was telling him the story as he escorted me out of the hot sun into the shade of the old church.

"Let's go inside for a while; it's getting hot out here with the sun coming up." Reverend Young had put his arms around my shoulder and guided me out of the cemetery toward the old church.

We went to the front of the church and sat in the first pew. It was cool inside with the breeze coming in through the windows. I rushed through the story with almost madness in my voice. He stared at me very attentively only reaching up to scratch his chin once or twice. I told him about the brooch and gloves being found in the old fireplace on Penn Road, Mrs. Davis' story about Daniel Brewer, and the fire that forced the Black people to move here on the banks of the river. I told him about the grave there at the Lazarus Tree, a mother, and child that died the same day as the other nine but buried apart from them. I told him, I believe, everything. He took in every word before he opened his mouth to speak.

"I, myself, am not from Oakman. I came from the North to pastor the Mount Zion Church. I have to tell you in my four years of living among these people I have never heard any story like this before. Of course, 1905 was a long time ago; even a person born in that year, wouldn't be much help, would be over eighty years old." He stared at the altar for a moment before continuing, "I don't know exactly why the truth of this story is important to you, Mr. Wallace, but I do know why it's significant to me and the Black people of Oakman, I'd like to help you find the truth if you would let me."

I nodded my appreciation and he continued.

"I don't know just what I can do for now except ask the members of my congregation about Pennsylvania and Daniel Brewer. Maybe they haven't told me this story because I haven't asked. Maybe they don't know it. I'll have to see. I do know that if the parents and grandparents of the Black people of Oakman felt the story was best left untold, just as the White people have apparently decided, there may be a very few who know it or will discuss it even now. I will find out all that I can at my end."

We both stood up from the pew at the same time, shaking hands and assuring one another that we would stay in touch. Reverend Young walked me back to the door of the church and stood in the door as I walked back to my car.

As I opened the door, I looked back at the Lazarus Tree one more time and noticed again something I had not noticed before. Some five or six feet off the ground were more rusty nails driven into the trunk of the tree. Where the nails were driven in, there was a rectangular shape indented in the bark of the tree. This one place the huge tree had seemed to age less than it had anywhere else. All I could think of was that at one time there must have been a sign attached to it. A sign that for some years had protected that one spot from the sun and rain that the rest of the tree had been exposed to continually since its birth. I could only imagine what the sign had said. I could see as I got in the car and backed out that the sign had been placed directly over the grave of the unknown mother and child.

12

I TRIED TO PHONE MRS. DAVIS SATURDAY AFTERNOON after returning home from Lazarus Cemetery. Sunday afternoon I went by and knocked on her front door. Both attempts to contact her were in vain. It was not until Monday afternoon that I went by her sizeable gothic house and found out what had become of her. It was about four-fifteen when I knocked on the door impatiently and then rang the angel bell as I had before. To my surprise, a rather large Black woman with an apron tied high above her waist threw back the door with a very loud and abrupt greeting.

"Miz Davis ain't here, and I can't help ya!" Her eyes and teeth were white as ivory, and there was a definite tone of anger or irritation in her greeting, I wasn't sure which.

I said, "My name is Bob Wallace. Mrs. Davis was trying to arrange a business meeting for me; I wonder if you might know when she will be in?" I said business meeting because this large, Black woman's tone and expression did not give the appearance that she would tolerate anything less.

She answered, "Not for a while, I 'spect. She in the hospital. Had a heart attack, bad one best I can tell."

I wondered for a moment why I had been so stupid not to think that Mrs. Davis might be ill and in the hospital. "Could you tell me her room number?" I asked, "how is she doing?"

She responded, "Room 119, but I 'spect it's different since they moved her up to Springhill."

They had moved her; she was, no doubt, very ill.

"How long ago did this happen? When did she go to the hospital?"

She had lowered her voice some, but her tone remained as irritated as before. "Don't know just when it happened. Sometimes last weekend. I found her there by the steps when I come in on Tuesday mornin. I wasn't here Monday – I had to go to the tooth dentist." She pointed over her shoulder at the staircase that ascended to the second floor. "She couldn't talk too good, but I got her up off that cold floor and took her to the couch to warm her up, then called the am-bo-lances. They was here pretty quick, too. All them lights agoin' roun'. Bells blastin' out, yes sir, it was somepin' to see."

I pictured in my mind this huge Black woman scooping Mrs. Davis up from the floor like a small child and walking her to the couch with no problem. This woman's arms were about the circumference of my legs. In my mind I was certain she could have carried me and Mrs. Davis to the couch.

"You gwine have to hurry up now, I got work to do. I been dustin' that there staircase half a day. Ain't a soul walked up it since Miz Laura came down it, and it had dust on it thick as my feet." I unconsciously looked down at her feet and doubted very seriously that dust could become that thick in a century, let alone a week!

"When was the last time you heard from her?"

She responded, "Well sir, she was in Oakman General til last Friday evenin'. I been goin' to see her every day til then. Goin' back in there where they keep them people that needs to be watched after more than the rest." I asked her if she meant intensive care. She responded stating, "Course, they wouldn't let me stay about ten minutes, seems to me she was getting' better. Course, lot can happen in a little while when your heart go bad. Miz Laura was talking pretty good by Thursday and Friday. Somepin' must have happened, though, cause they took her to Springhill in an airplane."

I tried to go back over the last few minutes of our conversation in my mind. I wondered in reference to the way Mrs. Davis was talking if the housekeeper was sure it was a heart attack and not a stroke, but I was afraid to question her knowledge at this point. She had calmed down considerably since first answering the door, and I had no desire to bring back the woman that had finished her first sentence with, "I can't help you."

I questioned, "Do you know which hospital Mrs. Davis is in at Springhill?"

"Didn't know they had more one up there. She in that big one that got the school for doctors in it."

University Hospital? I questioned her again. "Do you know if they will let her have visitors?"

She responded, "No sir, I haven't heard a word since Saturday morning, early. I came by here to crack the windows to let the house air. I was on my way to the hospital to see her. The hospital there in Springhill called on the phone and axed me about Miz Laura's next-a-kin. I thought she had done died in the night. Then they told me she was in Springhill and they needed to know who took care of her affairs. I told 'em up until now Miz Laura took care of her own affairs, didn't know 'bout no kin. Then they axes me if I'd look through her things and see if I could find out whom they might call about her. I told 'em I worked for Miz Laura Belle Davis about 12 years and I ain't never looked at her personal things, and ain't intendin' to start now."

I thought just a moment I might ask if I could come in and look for the name they needed, but then quickly dismissed the idea. After all, she had known Mrs. Davis for 12 years, and she wasn't going to look; she certainly was not likely to let me, whom she did not even know, past the front porch.

I asked, "Did they say how she was doing?"

She responded, "No sir, they just told me she was guarded. Guess that means they got nurses watchin' her door all the time. Musta got worse, tweren't nobody guardin' her up here in Oakman. I got to go back to work now, Miz Laura done paid me for the next two weeks, and it'll be all I can do to get all of this dust outa here by then. When nobody ain't home, a house gits dustier quicker than when somebody livin' right here in it." She started to close the door with her massive hands before I could think if there was anything else she might tell me. Just as the door began to close, I thought to ask her name.

"I'm sorry," I said, "I didn't catch your name."

"Froney, Froney Watkins." She was now standing behind the door as she closed it. "My daughter goin' to come with me tomorrow, help me call up there to Springhill. You stop by, and I'll tell you what they say."

She closed the door, but not nearly as abruptly as she opened it. Mrs. Watkins, I had decided, was not so rude as she was serious about giving Mrs. Davis her two weeks' worth even in her absence. Mrs. Watkins was perhaps more practical than I. She was keeping to the task she had been paid for and was not trying to think about Mrs. Davis' situation, which for now she could do absolutely nothing about. I returned to my car and thought all the way home about calling the hospital and finding out all that I could. If Mrs. Davis could see visitors, I was on my way to Springhill as soon as possible. I had only met her once, but I truly believed that at least a face she had seen once would be less frightening than so many she had never seen before.

I felt a strange, distressful urgency as I drove back home. The same feeling I had when my mother called ten years ago to tell me my father had suffered a stroke. I had only met Mrs.

Davis the one time, but I had the same tingling in my legs and feet I had experienced ten years ago. It is a desire to know about or see someone as fast as you can, then when you find out the truth, you wish you had not been in such a hurry in the first place. You want to know what their condition is, their chances of survival, but then when you find out the chances are not good, you wish, for just a few more days or hours, you had not known so you could remember them as they were.

There is some advantage for the living if they know someone they love is dying, rather than losing them suddenly. It gives those who will be left on earth a chance to say everything they have always wanted to say rather than wish for the rest of their lives that they had said it. That same feeling was overcoming me now, having found out that not only was Mrs. Davis ill, but so ill, in fact, that she had been moved to the largest hospital within two hundred miles. My reasons for feeling this urgency were selfish; deep down I knew that. It was not love or affection that made me feel this way; after all, I had only met her one time. It was instead, the feeling that I could have found out so much more, had I only stayed a while longer, or been more attentive, or more persistent about what I needed to know. I tried to convince myself that I cared for other reasons but honesty at this point was winning, at least, in my own mind.

As I came in the back door of the house, Mary met me in the kitchen to tell me that Tommy had been by to see me. I rushed past her to the phone in the den and didn't even acknowledge that I had heard her. Tommy had been entirely forgotten as having played any part in this whatsoever. His contribution was becoming more obscure with every passing day. I sat down and dialed directory assistance, waving a hand at Mary for her to stop talking as a recording on the other end recited the number for University Hospital. I dialed the number quickly, having to fend off Mary's questions one more time as the operator at the hospital answered the phone. I asked for the room of Mrs. Laura Davis.

There was a pause before she answered, "I'm sorry for the wait, sir, Mrs. Davis is in the Intensive Care Unit. I will ring the information nurse for the unit."

I do not think I had ever heard of an information nurse, let alone one that dealt with only one unit, but he or she should know what I needed to find out. The wait was longer this time before the woman answered.

"ICU information, Mrs. Kelly speaking. May I help you?"

"Yes," I responded, "I'm calling to inquire about Mrs. Laura Bell Davis."

She asked, "Your name please?"

I heard the distinct sound of fingers on a keyboard, no doubt, information being fed into a computer, and wondered if Mrs. Kelly was calling up Mrs. Davis' chart or adding my name to it.

"Robert Wallace," Mrs. Kelly questioned me, "Mr. Wallace, are you related to Mrs. Davis?" I thought for a moment before answering in an attempt to choose my words carefully. For a second

I thought I would lie, bettering my chances of getting information about her, but then I didn't.

"No, I am an acquaintance of Mrs. Davis. I have only recently discovered that she is ill. I wanted to inquire about her condition."

"Do you happen to know who her next-of-kin is?" She had completely ignored my question.

I responded, "To my knowledge, there is no next of kin."

Mrs. Kelly continued questioning me, "Do you perhaps know of an attorney, or someone, who handles her affairs?"

I told her, "No, to my knowledge, Mrs. Davis had handled her own affairs up until this time." That was the second time she had gotten that answer; it was the same one Froney Watkins had given the day before. There was another pause before I heard her voice again.

"Will you be visiting Mrs. Davis in the near future?"

"She can have visitors, then?"

Mrs. Kelly stated, "Yes, we have three times that a person may visit someone in ICU: 9:00 a.m., 1:00 p.m., and 6:00 p.m. With Mrs. Davis' condition, we would only allow a fifteen-minute visit each time."

Her 'condition' was why I had called in the first place. "Mrs. Kelly, what is Mrs. Davis' condition?"

She responded, "Ordinarily, we are not allowed to give out that information to anyone but immediate family, but it appears, Mr. Wallace, that you are as close as we may get. I have been trying to get information about relatives ever since Mrs. Davis was admitted but have gotten nowhere. The hospital there is Oakman has not been successful either. When did you think you might come to the hospital?"

I responded, "My plan is to be there for 9:00 visiting in the morning." However, I had not formulated a plan until that very moment.

Mrs. Kelly informed me, "I'm afraid Mrs. Davis is gravely ill. She has suffered a cerebrovascular accident or stroke. She has paralysis on her left side, and it is extremely difficult for her to speak. We believe from all indications that she suffered more than one such incident, perhaps several, since her condition declined after being admitted to Oakman Hospital. Our tests here indicate she has also had a heart attack in the past and this is of major concern, since we have not been able to completely stabilize her blood pressure and heart rate since her admission. These factors could cause another heart attack or stroke, so you can understand our concern with getting information about next-of-kin or a guardian of some kind. We would be very appreciative of any information about this matter that you could supply. To be honest, our information is so limited we do not even know her exact age."

I tried desperately to remember if Mrs. Davis had told me her age at our first and only meeting. There was, in my mind, some references in the conversation to her age but nothing that would help the hospital.

"I will certainly try to find out what I can, but I am afraid my only relationship has been with Mrs. Davis herself. I do know her husband has been dead for some time."

I did recall her pointing to the picture over the fireplace and saying it as her husband, and that he was dead. How long he had been dead, I really had no idea, but I had to say something that would lead away from the fact that I had only met her once.

"Well, Mr. Wallace," said Mrs. Kelly, "I'm afraid that Mrs. Davis will probably not be able to respond very well, if at all. But a familiar face certainly cannot hurt. My name is Caroline Kelly. When you do come in, I'd appreciate it if you would stop by my office on your way in. My office is right inside the ICU waiting room; my name is on the door."

"I will, thank you very much for talking with me." I hung up the phone but was thinking about where I might find out something more than what I knew about Mrs. Davis. Her house, of course, but Froney Watkins was guarding it, and I stood a better chance of getting into Fort Knox. Mary came back into the room with a cup of coffee. Although she had not asked, I knew she was waiting for me to explain my abrupt entrance.

Mary's patience had been without fault. When I stopped to think for a moment, I realized I had not included her in the search. I supposed she was keeping up with the journal, but I had forgotten about it in the last few days. Now she was sitting across from me, hearing only half of what I said on the phone and waiting for me to tell her the rest. Now that I thought about the situation, I realized I had not discussed Lazarus Cemetery with her at all. I really could not recall what I had done Saturday evening or Sunday, but I am sure I had not told her anything about Mrs. Davis, the one sound source other than Reverend Young that Mary had worked so hard to find.

My mind flashed back to my conversation with Froney Watkins for just a moment before I began to bring Mary up-to-date. Mrs. Watkins had said she found Mrs. Davis at the foot of the stairs on Tuesday morning. I took some comfort recalling that it had been last Monday that I had my meeting with Mrs. Davis. Froney had said it must have happened sometime over the weekend, but it couldn't have. Mrs. Davis had to have fallen sometime Monday night or Tuesday morning. At least I knew that she had not spent the entire weekend lying alone there on the floor. I thought for a moment I might call the house and tell Froney what I had remembered, but Mary was waiting, it was after five by now. Froney had probably left already anyway.

Mary broke into my thoughts from across the room asking, "What happened to Mrs. Davis?"

"She has had a stroke. They transferred her to University Hospital at Springhill. According to them, she is very ill."

Mary asked, "How did you find out about this?"

I responded, "Her housekeeper, Froney Watkins. She was there cleaning house when I came by this afternoon. She found Mrs. Davis last Tuesday morning lying on the floor. She was here in Oakman until this past Friday or Saturday, but she got worse. As far as I can tell from the nurse there in Springhill, Mrs. Davis is no better, if anything she is worse."

"When will you go to see her?" There was the approval, without question, that was always present in Mary's voice.

I responded, "Tomorrow. I can visit at nine a.m. I'd like to try and be there before then to talk to the nurses."

Mary asked, "Would you like for me to go with you?"

"No, as a matter of fact, I have another job for you to do here. One, I need for you to call in for me in the morning. Tell them anything. I do not like to lie, but I have time off coming, and there is no way to explain this to anyone."

Mary asked, "What is the second thing I need to do?"

"The hospital is having no luck at all in findings any relatives of Mrs. Davis'. I need for you to go over to her house and see if you can get past Froney. See if she will let you in to look at an address book, mail, something that might give us a clue about whom to call to make decisions about Mrs. Davis' care. Froney stood at the front door like a sentinel when I was there, but she might feel more comfortable with a woman. She also told me her daughter would be with her tomorrow. That might loosen her up some."

A genuine expression of sorrow came over Mary's face before she spoke, "You mean she is up there all alone? She had a stroke over a week ago, and they still have not found anyone who knows her?"

I answered Mary, "Apparently, no one except me. I have not told them or Froney and that I only met the woman one time; for now, we had both better keep that to ourselves. Strange though, I was under the impression she had lived in Oakman her whole life. Funny, no one at the hospital here knew a relative to contact."

Mary asked me, "What time do you want me to go to her house?"

I told her, "Well, I'm only guessing, but I assume Froney gets there by eight; she was still there working today past four."

Now that Mrs. Davis' situation was understood, I thought I would move on to Lazarus Cemetery. I described to Mary the cemetery and the tree in its entirety. I tried to focus on the relationship between the nine graves and the one containing the mother and child. I tried desperately to create a relationship between them in my own mind I knew might not exist, all the while knowing I still needed to look at the *War and Peace* to even begin to put the two together. Without Mrs. Davis, that was at the least going to be a much more difficult task than it had been when she was well. I had to fight hard with my conscience to decide if I was going to see Mrs. Davis because she needed me or because I needed her. I was hoping, even though the situation changed a great deal in a short time, we still needed each other.

I asked Mary, "What did Tommy have to say?"

She answered me by stating, "Nothing really; he just wanted to talk. Mostly the same old things. His father is working him to death, they lost this contract and so forth, you know, same song. He did say Jack was curious what you were looking for in the records room. He saw your name on the register. I told Tommy I didn't know. I figured the less Jack Morrow knew, the better. Tommy said the map book Jack was looking for was gone from the shelves. He cursed the clerk out about it, Tommy said, but they are probably used to that by now."

I asked, "What book was he looking for?"

She responded, "1905, according to Tommy. Something about the city postponing the contract on the new library there on Penn Road."

I got up and walked into the kitchen. I picked up the spiral notebook that had become our journal of the story that was so carefully hiding or being hidden from us and turned back to the first few pages.

"The 1905 record book? It was there less than a month ago. April eleventh to be exact."

13

I LEFT TOO EARLY FOR SPRINGHILL AS LACK OF PATIENCE overcame me again. I didn't even wake Mary when I left at five-thirty a.m. She knew what she had to do, and I had no doubt that she would do it. I drove slowly, daydreaming along the way; trying again to piece it all together and find more common ground. I was certain Mrs. Davis could have supplied it, and I wondered as the early morning traffic passed me by if I should have told her the whole truth. Maybe I should have shown her the brooch. She might have known exactly whose initials were R.L.G. It was too late for that now, and I had to have some feeling for Mrs. Davis' illness, some compassion for her altered state. Too many questions might overwhelm her. She might, in her mind, want to answer but her body might not allow it. Such an internal dilemma might possibly be the cause of her demise. No matter what feelings I did or did not have for Laura Belle Davis, I had no desire to be the cause of her death.

The building was easily found, one of the largest buildings in town. As I drove down the off-ramp marked 'University Hospital,' the huge building easily came into view even though it was several blocks away. On the way down University Boulevard, there was every kind of health care service imaginable. These services ran all the way up to the parking lot of the huge hospital complex. I drove through the toll gate, pulled the parking ticket,and found my way to a parking place somewhere on one of the upper decks. I sat with the motor running for several seconds, thinking that I might not get out, that I might just back out and go home. I questioned why I had even come and if I really had the right to do so. I barely knew her, and again I was wrestling with my conscience for an unselfish reason to be here.

On my way across the parking lot, I noticed a helicopter pad and I realize this was Froney's 'airplane which brought Mrs. Davis to Springhill. As I walked to the elevator I could see I was very right about leaving too early; it was only seven a.m. Two hours until the first visiting time. Eight a.m. would undoubtedly be the earliest that I could see Caroline Kelly. I made my way to the ground floor and wandered into the cafeteria, which was just opening, and sat down to think over a cup of coffee. I had been sitting for perhaps ten minutes when a young woman, perhaps thirty-five years old with short, brown, hair sat down at the table directly across from me. She was wearing street clothes and a long white lab coat. Her identification badge was clipped to the lapel of her coat and was as plain from this distance as if I were sitting at the table with her: **Caroline Kelly, RN, ICU DON,** which I took to be the Director of Nursing. Had I leaned over any farther, my chest would have been covering my coffee cup. I felt my mouth hanging open, and I stared very strangely. How could this be? There were fourteen floors to this building, 1400 beds. How could it be that one of the two people I had come here to see had sat down four feet in front of me two hours before I was supposed to see her?

It was too late now; she had seen my stare. I had no choice but to introduce myself or have her call the security guard standing at the door where I had come in.

"Mrs. Kelly, please excuse my stare. I was startled by the coincidence of meeting here. I'm Robert Wallace. I spoke to you in the phone yesterday about Mrs. Laura Davis, a patient of yours in ICU."

After listening to my speech and pondering for a few seconds, she smiled and invited me to her table. "Of course, have a seat, Mr. Wallace. You have come rather early, haven't you? Visiting hours are an hour and a half away."

I answered, "Yes, I'm afraid I have arrived long before time. I was so eager to get here I left much sooner than I meant to. How was Mrs. Davis' night?"

Caroline answered, "To be honest; I haven't been to the floor yet. When I left at five-thirty yesterday, she was no better, no worse. You did tell me you were not related to her, didn't you?" I felt a coldness in her voice that was there when we spoke on the phone, but I had not recognized it before. I wondered now if she had a genuine desire to locate a relative for Mrs. Davis' benefit or whether there was a lot more paperwork involved in sending a body to the morgue when there was no one else to sign the release.

Caroline Kelly appeared much more businesslike now than she had on the phone. Even her smile was pasted on; it disappeared the minute she began to speak. I thought at first I might lash back at her verbally, but that would not help Mrs. Davis or me.

"No, I am afraid I am just a friend. My wife is going to her house today to see if her housekeeper will let her look through her things to see if she might find out some information from you."

Caroline responded by stating, "That would be Mrs. Watkins. I spoke with her on the phone; she was no help at all." The coolness was growing worse now that I had brought Froney into the conversation. Froney had dealt with Mrs. Kelly without regard to her position as a "director" and it was obvious she did not like it. Caroline continued, "I tried to explain the situation to that woman, but she simply refused to listen."

I could easily see that Caroline had repressed a racial slur in her reference to Froney although clearly, race had nothing whatsoever to do with Froney's obvious territorial feeling about Mrs. Davis and her house. I wished for a moment I had brought Froney with me and let her personally explain how she felt about going through her employer's things. I felt certain she would have made it much clearer for Ms. Kelly in person. Again, I thought I might lash out, but I didn't. Instead, I asked Ms. Kelly, "Is there any chance that Mrs. Davis will be able to regain some function, with therapy or something?"

Ms. Kelly stated, "I have to have someone to sign for therapy, Mr. Wallace. You see, that is the gist of the problem. We need proof of insurance, some guarantee of payment, and someone to sign for responsibility. Without it, you see, we are limited with our options for treatment." Now came the truth. Ms. Kelly was a nurse in title only. She was actually a bill collector. An 'information nurse' who obtained information about where to send the bills. She obviously supervised care based on ability to pay. When she discovered Mrs. Davis had a Black housekeeper, it had undoubtedly increased Ms. Kelly's agony. She felt certain that Mrs. Davis could pay if only it was known where to send the bills. Ms. Kelly stood up from the table to make her way to her office, and there was a hint of frost in the air.

Ms. Kelly said, "It will still be quite some time before we begin our first visiting hour. No need to hurry." While her lips did not move, I felt her say, "And since you cannot sign for her, you will not get in one minute earlier."

She turned and walked out of the door without ever looking back. Now I had the feeling I was looking for, genuine concern for Mrs. Davis' wellbeing.

Nine o'clock came more quickly than I thought it would. I was standing outside the ICU door just as the sign on the wall instructed me to do. I had passed Ms. Kelly's office door on the way here. It was closed, and I had not knocked. The sign on the wall said to form a single line. I was the line! There had been no one in the waiting room when I arrived and therefore no one to form a line with. At precisely nine a.m., on the waiting room clock, a young nurse in a spotless uniform appeared at the door.

"Who do you wish to see?" I answered and she opened the door back and allowed me to enter, saying, "cubicle four", as I passed. I moved down the row of glass-enclosed rooms on my right and counted to myself, I not noticed the numbers were clearly inscribed on each one.

I saw only one other patient as I moved, a little, tightly-drawn man in the first room. If he was breathing, I had not detected it as I moved by. I felt the young nurse that had opened the door at my back as I came to the number four on the glass window. Through the window was Mrs. Davis, and at first, all I could do was stare. I had never in my life seen so much change in such a brief time! When I last saw Mrs. Davis, her hair was set and styled; now it stuck out in every direction, what there was of it. Her silver hair had seemed much thicker before. Her skin had darkened, and the lines I had seen on her face before were now like furrows in a field waiting to be planted. There were dark circles under her eyes, and the one arm that extended down by her right side was covered with green and purple bruises. The nurse allowed me to take a breath for a minute at the door before she placed her hand on my shoulder and directed me to Mrs. Davis' bedside.

The nurse said, "Go on in, I'm sure she needs a friendly face. If you have any questions, I'll be right out here at the desk."

Coming close to Mrs. Davis' bed made it even worse. Everything I had seen from a few feet away was only magnified on close observation. There was a plastic IV line running under the cover at the foot of the bed which explained the bruises on her arm; they had used it up. Monitors on two walls jumped and beeped with her heart, and her left arm and hand were curled inward and upward toward her chin. A washcloth had been rolled up and placed in her contracted left hand to keep her fingernails from digging into her palm, and a towel had been placed under the left side of her head to catch the saliva that trickled from her mouth. I wondered again as I gripped the side rail of her bed what I was doing here. Mrs. Davis could not help me, and I most definitely could not help her.

I leaned over the bed rail to call her name, but stopped, wondering for a moment if I should. People talk to people in this condition all the time. I, myself, talked with my own father for several minutes after he was most likely dead. I had read somewhere before his death that hearing is always the last of the senses to leave you. Leaning closely, I detected a foul odor coming from her mouth as she exhaled. I called her name in almost a whisper, "Mrs. Davis, Mrs. Davis, it's me, Bob Wallace."

Her eyes popped open immediately. The right side of her mouth curled up in a smile, although the left side remained straight and continued to dribble. She attempted to bring her hand across her abdomen, but the movement was too spastic and weak. I reached and grabbed her hand and held it tightly although she was not able to hold pressure on mine. Her mouth came open and sounds and moisture came out. I was glad I had come as she began to speak in a slow but clear tone.

"I didn't tell all…the truth." Her eyes closed, and she licked her lips before she continued. "Go to the *War and Pea..ce*…look for Harlan Smartt and Na…Na…Nathan Sawyer, the fire that bur…was no accident." She closed her eyes and breathed deeply before she continued. "I can't tel yo…you all the truth, I don't know it all, but its there in the pa…per. People should know the truth." She batted her eyes as if she might pass out, but she spoke one more time. "Harlan Smart…tt, Sheriff Harlan Smar…."

Mrs. Davis fell back sound asleep as if the few words she spoke had drained her completely. She let go of the weak grasp she had on my hand as the nurse informed me that my time was up for now. The time had passed quickly. I must have stared at her pitiful state longer than I thought. I walked back out to the waiting room and sat with the back page of a magazine facing me and wrote everything she had said, paying particular attention to the names, 'Sheriff Harlan Smartt' and 'Nathan Sawyer.' When I got through, I walked back to the door of ICU and lightly knocked on the door. The same nurse that had led me to Mrs. Davis' bedside answered again, "I was wondering if I might see her again at one p.m.?"

The nurse answered stating, "To be honest, I do not think she is up to it. That talk you two just had is the most activity Mrs. Davis has had since her stroke, and she was having some erratic heart activity while you were in there. I would have called you out sooner, but that's the longest she's kept her eyes open since she got here, and I really hated to cut her off from your company. Why don't you come back in the morning? Maybe, she will be more rested, and her heart will have slowed down some."

I responded stating, "Can I leave my name and number for you to call if she needs anything?"

The nurse answered, "Sure, come on back to the desk."

I followed her back to the desk, recited the number to her, and gave her my name. As I turned to walk back out, I took one last look at Mrs. Davis' frail body behind the glass. She was fast asleep.

"We will call you if her condition changes, Mr. Wallace. Don't worry; we'll take good care of her for you."

As I walked out of the ICU by Ms Kelly's office I saw the door was open about halfway. I slowed down just on the other side of Ms. Kelly's door to hear her say into the phone, "She's fine, Mrs. Watkins, now have you been able to come up with a name for me yet?" Froney was on the phone just as she had said she would be, and Caroline Kelly was using the same arrogant tone she undoubtedly used on Saturday with Froney. I should have informed her status and tone would have no effect on the outcome of her conversation with Ms. Froney Watkins.

14

I RECEIVED A CALL FROM UNIVERSITY HOSPITAL AT two-forty a.m. on May 11, 1988. They informed me that Mrs. Davis had passed away after having suffered another more damaging stroke. After the first nurse finished telling me about Mrs. Davis, a second one cut in on the line.

"Mr. Wallace, this is Joan Kent. I was wondering if you might come up and sign Mrs. Davis' final paperwork?"

"What sort of paperwork?"

"Her final bill, release to a funeral home, insurance claims form, a few things to finalize her hospital stay." I remember thinking as I hung up the phone without answering her, Caroline Kelly has an alter ego name Joan Kent that works the graveyard shift...

I did not go to work on Wednesday, if for no other reason than I did not want to. I called the plant and explained that there had been a death in the family. Froney had allowed Mary into Mrs. Davis' home the day before, but the search was in vain and would have been even if Mrs. Davis had not passed away in the night. There was nothing, Mary explained, that would lead one to a next of kin, a relative of any kind, close or distant. Life had apparently consisted of Mrs. Davis and, up until his death, her husband, whose name was Gerald. Then her life consisted of her and Froney. It appeared from all indications that other than Froney, Mrs. Davis had very little contact with the outside world for the past ten or twelve years. Froney appeared to know very little about her employer. Froney did, however, know Mr. Davis' name and that he died shortly before she came to work for Mrs. Davis.

I was at a standstill on what to do, if anything, about Mrs. Davis' demise. I did feel like I owed it to Froney to go by this morning and tell her that Mrs. Davis had passed away. When I did, she cried as she continued to clean, assuring me that 'Miz Laura' had paid her for two weeks in advance, and Froney fully intended to finish it out. When I returned home from consoling

Froney, I was elated to find that Mrs. Davis had reached out from death to help me. A Mrs. Oscar Stokes had called to say that he was in charge of the *Somerville War and Peace* collection, and that he received a letter of introduction from Mrs. Davis the week before. He would be glad, he told Mary, to arrange for me to 'view' the collection as soon as I wished.' Mrs. Davis must have written the letter and placed it in her box the same day we met. For that, I thanked her in my heart knowing it was too late to thank her any other way.

Before returning Mrs. Stokes' call, I struggled unsuccessfully with what to tell him about Mrs. Davis' death. After all, if the knowledge of her death might have some ill effect on her introduction, that would be no help to me in fulfilling her last request, to find out the truth. I really had not decided what to say when I dialed his number, but soon discovered I had no choice but to relay the information to him. "Mrs. David wrote me that she intended to come with you to Sommerville. Is that still her plan?" He had left me no way out. "I'm sorry, Mr. Stokes, but Mrs.

Davis passed away last night. She had a stroke ten days or so ago and never really recovered. She died in the night at University Hospital in Springhill. She was transferred there as her condition worsened last week."

"Oh, I'm sorry, that is a shame," said Mr. Stokes. "So, you'll be coming alone then?" Mrs. Davis' death had very little effect, if any, on my seeing the papers. I realized without his saying so that she it was as a celebrated member of the Wayne County Historical Society that Mrs. Davis had written to Mr. Stokes, not as someone he really knew personally.

"Mr. Stokes, would it be possible for me to bring my wife with me to help with my research?" He told me it would be fine, and we arranged to meet at the Sommerville Courthouse at nine o'clock a.m.

on Saturday, May 21. That was over a week away. I had hoped for something sooner, but I was not, at this point, inclined to try and persuade him otherwise.

The ten days before my meeting with Mr. Stokes went by slowly. I did very little other than add Mrs. Davis' death, and the circumstances surrounding it, to the journal. Tommy had been by twice to talk. Again, there was nothing except his ever-deteriorating relationship with his father. I thought I might ask Tommy if he wanted to come to Sommerville with us, but I had asked for permission for only one other and wanted nothing to stand in the way of my seeing those newspapers. He asked about the brooch and gloves, and I told him I discovered nothing new about them, which was true. Their part in all of this was becoming more obscure with every passing day. Reverend Young had called once to tell me nothing except that his parishioners had been very closed-mouth about their ancestors migration from Penn Road to the river, but that he would continue to ask questions.

I went to work every day, sat at my desk, and did virtually nothing but attempt to pass the time until Saturday. Mr. Stokes called me on Friday, and I held my breath as he spoke, thinking he was calling to cancel, but, quite the contrary, he was calling to confirm our appointment.

Mary and I started out about seven thirty, stopping for coffee along the way, driving slowly, and taking in the view. As we drove down Main Street in Sommerville, we looked without commenting at the abandoned and decaying store fronts on either side of the road. On the left side of the road, there was a cotton gin that had long ago become a haven for rats, probably feeding on the rotten remains of cotton seed that had fallen through the floor. There was an old wooden post office, on the corner across the street from the Courthouse, that was flying an American flag by the front door. It appeared to be the only commercial building where some business, however limited, was still carried on.

We pulled in front of the two-story, red brick building at about eight a.m. and looked out the windshield at the small dome that still adorned the roof. The flagpole rising from the dome was still intact, and I could imagine a Confederate flag flapping in the wind though no flag had flown from the roof of this building in a long, long time.

Mrs. Stokes arrived on foot about eight forty-five, made his introduction, and escorted us through the front door of the Courthouse which he had an extremely tough time unlocking. He had us wait in a small foyer while he went behind a counter to open the huge door of the safe behind it. Mr. Stokes was a very tall, frail-looking man with balding grey hair. His clothes fit very loosely on his body. He carried on his belt a ring of keys that looked on first observation like they had not opened anything in years. A longer look revealed five or six keys among the others that might be less than fifty years old. He called us back to the door of the vault and began with a very businesslike tone giving us his obviously rehearsed instructions never mentioning Mrs. Davis.

"The stacks of papers begin on the left-hand side with the first year of publication which was 1850. Each stack represents one decade of the paper's existence. Up until 1860, the paper only came out once a month. Beginning in sixty, it became a weekly paper and continued to be so until it went out of business in 1917, which is the last stack here on my right." He took two or three shallow breaths and continued. "The papers have been placed between pieces of clear plexiglass. Beside each stack is an empty space. If you would simply start by putting each paper and the plastic sheet with the date on it face down as you go through, the papers can be easily restacked in order by just returning them to their face-up position. When you find an edition you wish to look through, just place it on the table there in the middle of the vault, and when you are through, return it to the stack facing down before you continue. Are there any questions?"

I felt like I had just heard recorded instructions about something I had ordered from a mail order house. Something ordered from a toll-free number that nobody needs. Mrs. Stokes' tone changed completely after he finished his initial instructions.

"I'll be checking on you from time to time. If you should decide to leave when I'm not here, I would appreciate it if one of you would

89

walk up the street to my house and let me know before leaving. I live in a dark green two-story house just one block up Lee Street from the Courthouse. I'll be in my yard or around the house all day." He pointed out the west window of the room we were in indicating the direction of Lee Street. How hard could it be to find, there were only four streets in Sommerville, and all of them converged on one side or the other of the Courthouse.

Mr. Stokes left out of the same door we had come in without ever actually entering the vault. I wondered as I stared at the huge steel door to the vault why he had us wait in the next room while he opened it. Two large iron hasps had been welded to the door and the frame, so the door could be secured with two equally large keyed locks. The dial that at one time held the combination to the door had been removed and was nowhere in sight.

Mary and I knew as we moved into the vault what we were looking for. I would have loved to start at the beginning and go through every paper until the end, but there was not time. I had no idea if this would be my first and last look at the *War and Peace*. I did not really know if the introduction from Mrs. Davis was a one-time thing or if it gave the holder unlimited access to the papers. I was going to treat this as my first and last view and just look for what I can to see.

We started with the stack marked 'January 3, 1901', placing the papers face down with the sheet of plastic embossed with the month and week between them just as Mr. Stokes had instructed us to do. Each paper consisted of roughly four to six pages about half the size of a modern-day daily newspaper. Each paper bore the heading *In War and Peace* across the top of the front page. The stories were short and very seldom needed to be continued on the next page. There were hand-drawn advertisements throughout for everything from 'Vegacal for the Bile' to a 'Hercules Shotgun' that was more powerful than all the rest.

15

IT WAS IN THE EDITION FOR THE FIRST WEEK IN MAY of 1901 that I began to find what Mrs. Davis had told me to look for as well as secrets she had not revealed. On the front page of that issue was a black and white photograph of a large man in a derby, flanked on either side by two young girls. The headline read *Oakman Council Appoints Smartt Sheriff*. A few sentences under the photograph made me look at the young girls extremely hard.

> "The newly appointed Sheriff Smartt was accompanied to the swearing-in ceremony by his two young daughters, 13-year-old Mollie Jean, and 4-year-old Laura Belle. Mrs. Smartt is deceased."

I leaned over and looked at the photograph very intently. Even at four years old there was no mistaking that this young girl was either Laura Bell Davis, whom I had seen only twice or very closely related to her. The resemblance of this petite four-year-old, clutching her father's hand to Mrs. Davis was uncanny. If it were she, she had changed extraordinarily little in the past eighty-seven years. Other than the fact that she had grown taller and older, she looked the same. I had to go over the numbers in my head several times before I could produce Mrs. Davis' age when she died over a week ago. If this little girl was, in fact, the Laura Belle I knew, she was ninety-one at her death. I pictured in my mind her frail face at the hospital in Springhill and realized she could have been one hundred and ninety-one for all I knew. I know the stroke seemed to age her excessively since we first met.

I wondered why Mrs. Davis had not given me this information

before. She had to know I would not overlook her in the photograph with the man she had told me to look for. We continued through the stack of newspapers marked '1901-1910.' There were several stories about the illustrious career of Sheriff Smartt. The front page of the September 1901 issue was filled with the assassination of President McKinley. Other news events were covered accordingly, but we hastened through looking for more of the information we had come here to find.

It was the issue for the third week in February of 1905 that we found the second name Mrs. Davis had related to me. 'Local Colored Youth Taken into Custody for Rape.' In smaller print, under the headline, was a further explanation:

"Nathan Sawyer was taken into custody today for the rape of Miss Mollie Jean Smartt, the daughter of Oakman Sheriff, Harlan Smartt. Sawyer was arrested by federal marshals at Sheriff Smartt's request. Smartt stated that he did not want to interfere with the prosecution of this man for the rape of his daughter and asked that Sawyer be taken into custody by federal marshals and moved to another county for his own safety. Sheriff Smartt stated that he did not want to be accused of interfering with due process of this Colored boy's trial. Miss Smartt is recovering from the attack at her father's home, and he has asked that reporters not attempt to contact her concerning this case."

There was a small article in the lower left corner of the May 1, 1905 issue telling of Nathan Sawyer's fate. No other news was printed before this.

"Nathan Sawyer was today found guilty of the rape of Miss Mollie Jean Smartt, of Oakman Sheriff, Harlan Smartt's daughter. Sawyer had been sentenced to life in prison and will be transferred within the week to the state prison at Poplar Bluff. Sawyer was tried at the Baldwin County Courthouse where he has been held since his arrest in Oakman last February. Sheriff Smartt was interviewed at his office after hearing the news. He stated he was glad he had asked for the youth to be moved out of Wayne County, so there could be no accusations of interference or biased with the trial. Sheriff Smartt further stated that he had been confident of the verdict all along".

The next article we needed was found in the issue for the first week of July 1905. It was the first time since her rape and the arrest of Nathan Sawyer that Mollie Jean Smartt was mentioned again.

"A valley-wide search begins today for Mollie Jean Smartt, the seventeen-year old daughter of Oakman Sheriff, Harlan Smartt. Sheriff Smartt told authorities that he put his daughter on the three-o-clock train for Nashville on July 4, 1905. He was sending her to visit her aunt since Miss Smartt had recently been despondent over her attack by Nathan Sawyer in February of this year. Sheriff Smartt stated that his daughter had not left the house since her attack, and he was trying to get her away from Oakman to see if she could get over her fear. He did not discover that Mollie Jean had never arrived at his sister's house, or the depot, in Nashville until July 7th. He was occupied with the fire that destroyed the Colored section of Oakman known to those people as 'Pennsylvania,' and did not receive word from his sister until the morning of July 7th, at which time he contacted both Alabama and Tennessee authorities to aid him in the search for his daughter. Sheriff Smartt set out on horseback on the seventh in an attempt to retrace his daughter's trail."

A few lines on the bottom of the front page directed the reader to the *News for the Colored* for more details about the fire. This section of the paper was found in the back of the paper in the lower right-hand part of the page. I thought, as I turned the pages to the back that the *War and Peace* must have been quite a progressive paper to have such a section at all in 1905, even though it was on the back page of the paper. There under the heading *News for the Colored*, appeared a short article about the fire.

> "A fire broke out in the Colored section of Oakman some time during the night of July 4 or the morning of July 5. It was rumored that the fire may have been started by Colored youths attempting to shoot fireworks stolen from the Oakman July 4 celebration. The fire, which raged most of the night totally destroyed the Colored section of town known as 'Pennsylvania.' Local residents spent the night attempting to control and contain the fire. It is believed that as many as nine residents have perished in the blaze. Exact numbers are not known since the Colored continue to dig out from under the tragedy of the fire."

There were the date and the number I had found at Lazarus Cemetery, July 4, 1905! The people under the tombstones at the Cemetery had not died of an illness as Reverend Young thought; they had died in the fire that destroyed their homes! They had all even been accounted for early on, except for the mother and child. Their fate was nowhere to be found, not in the *War and Peace* anyway.

Over the next several months, and even years, there were stories that became shorter and less frequent with the passing of time about the disappearance of Mollie Jean Smartt. Those articles came to an end with the death of Harlan Smartt in July of 1908. *"Sheriff Harlan Smartt Found Dead at His Home."*

> "Sheriff Harlan Smartt was found dead today at his home in Oakman by local deputy Percy Stanley. Smartt had been despondent over the disappearance of his elder daughter some three years ago. He spent many hours of his last year searching for her, but to date, she has never been found. Foul play is not suspected in the death of Sheriff Smartt."

The article went on to recount the details of Mollie Jean's disappearance on her way to her aunt's home in Nashville. The article also included details of her rape by Nathan Sawyer and his subsequent conviction and life sentence. The article never made any references to why or how Sheriff Smartt died. Other than the reference to Sheriff's 'elder daughter,' indicating there was more than one, Laura Belle was not mentioned in any of the articles, since the Sheriff's appointment when she was four years old.

As Mary and I continued to turn through the stacks, we realized that with Sheriff Smartt's death came an end to any more news about him, Mollie Jean, Nathan Sawyer, or the fire that destroyed Pennsylvania. I walked up to Mr. Stokes house and found him sitting in a swing on his front porch. He returned with me to lock the vault. We thanked him for his time, and he invited us back any time, as long as we called ahead.

On the drive back home, neither Mary nor I spoke. We were exhausted with the new revelations we had discovered. I had gone to Sommerville in an attempt to make some real headway in my search. I had not known until we examined the *War and Peace* that our quest had just begun. Mrs. Davis was more a part of this than she had led me to believe. For some reason, she would rather the truth be told by someone other than herself. If Laura Bell Smartt Davis knew the entire truth, she had taken it with her to her grave.

About the only fact I confirmed by going to Sommerville was that the nine people buried together at Lazarus Cemetery had died in the fire that burned Pennsylvania. Other than that, I had only opened several new doors, none of which appeared to point me toward my original goal, the owner of the brooch.

Now, Mary, had her work cut out for her. Nathan Sawyer's trial was perhaps at the top of the list. Harlan Smartt must have been one hell of a man to protect the rights of the Black man that raped the Sheriff's own daughter in 1905. He could have just shot Sawyer in the street, and no one would have blamed Smartt. He would have no doubt been elected Sheriff time and time again because of it. After all, this was the South in 1905, and he was 'The Law'. Who would have stopped him, let alone advise him to be careful to protect this young Black man's rights?

We needed to know if any record of Nathan Sawyer's trials still existed in some basement archive in Baldwin County. We further needed to know his eventual fate. I assumed for that we needed to contact the state prison system. Like every other aspect of this story, time would undoubtedly play a significant role. So much of it had passed it was impossible to know if any record had been kept at the time, let alone preserved for the future, of the fate of a poor Black boy who raped a white girl. The *War and Peace* had dealt with his fate as little as possible; that was obvious. They had reported just enough to let the people know he had been dealt with; whether this punishment fit the crime, as far as the general public was concerned, remained to be seen.

Then, of course, there was a question of what Miss Laura Bell Smartt Davis had done from the age of eleven on. She was four years old at the time her father was nominated sheriff, and he had died seven years later. Her mother was already dead. Even her older sister had been missing three years. Where Laura had gone, and what she had done all her life was of major importance to me. Of course, there was the truth she had asked me to find, the truth she had only known part of. Mrs. Davis had been in possession of the truth ninety-one years. Why had she left it to me to bring that truth to light, someone she barely knew. I felt some small hint of anger at her for leaving it to me to find. These new revelations, for the time being, only added to the feelings of hopelessness I had felt before. Now I needed to know about Sheriff Smartt, Mollie Jean, Nathan, and Laura Belle Smartt Davis. So much time had passed, it was hard to know where to begin.

Sunday passed quickly. Mary and I had passed the time discussing who or what agency to write first. Mary did compose and mail two carefully worded letters, one to the Baldwin County Courthouse, and one to the prison system. It was late Sunday afternoon when a break came I had not expected, and one that would at least answer some of my questions.

At 5:30, I received a person-to-person call from William L. Phillips, Attorney at Law.

"Mr. Wallace, please."

"Speaking."

"Mr. Robert Wallace?"

"Yes."

He had an even tone to his voice, not high or low. I could almost see through the phone there was no expression on his face. He talked slowly, with a very definite Southern drawl.

"Mr. Wallace, this is Bill Phillips. I'm a lawyer down here in Cornerville. I'm trying to get some information on the death of Mrs. Laura Bell Davis. Mrs. Davis was really a client of my father's. He retired some years ago, and I have since taken over his practice. To tell you the truth, I didn't know she was a client of my father until I received a letter from someone there in Oakman last week."

My heart stopped for a moment, thinking that there was someone in Oakman who did know about Mrs. Davis' life before, but the excitement was short-lived.

Mr. Phillips informed me, "You see, last week I received an anonymous letter informing me that University Hospital at Springhill was looking for information about Mrs. Davis' affairs. I contacted the hospital, and they told me they had run an ad in the Oakman paper for information about Mrs. Davis. Their records listed you and a Mrs. Froney Watkins as her only contacts while she was in the hospital, and I was wondering what light you might shed on this situation. To be quite honest, I was wondering if you might have been the one who sent this letter to me, or should I say sent it to my father?"

I had to choose my words carefully. This was an attorney that had no reason to tell me anything, but he wanted to know what I knew, which was almost nothing. I had to be careful, so I could arrange a trade of information without his knowing it.

"I'm sorry Mr. Phillips, but my only acquaintance with Mrs. Davis was here in Oakman. Why did she have an attorney down in Cornerville?" I had no idea what his answer would be. None of your damn business came to mind, but after all, he had nothing to lose, as far as I know by telling me about her past life, if he knew.

Mr. Phillips questioned me, "You didn't know Mrs. Davis before she came back to Oakman?" 'Came back,' that was the part of the information I was looking for.

I answered, "No, I'm afraid I didn't."

Mr. Phillips continued, "To be honest; my information comes from my father, whose mind is not as sharp as it used to be. He is actually the one who knew Mrs. Davis. I talked to him when I received the letter from Oakman. Seems like Mr. Davis lost her parents as a child. There was no family to take her in, and she was placed in what at that time was the State Home for Children at Monroe, which is just down the road, about ten miles, from Cornerville. She grew up there, never being adopted. When she became an adult, she came here to Monroe College and became a teacher, returning to teach at the children's home. Eventually, she became superintendent of the home. Gerald Davis became a teacher there many years later, and they eventually married late in life for both of them, I understand. She retired around the age of sixty, and they returned to her family home there in Oakman. Seems the house she lived in as a child had been taken by the city for back taxes. She and Mr. Davis made a trip back there after they married. My father believes that this was the first time she had been back to Oakman since she left as a child."

I could hear the shuffling of papers from his end of the phone, and he paused for a moment before he continued.

"A child of eleven, as a matter of fact. They bought the house from the city and had it restored, and eventually retired there. My father, William L. Phillips, Sr., was there lawyer when they lived here at Cornerville, and they simply never retained another one.
For what reason, I don't know." Again, there was the shuffling or thumbing through of some kind of paperwork. Mr. Phillips continued, "According to my father's records, he only saw Mrs. Davis one more time. She came here to Monroe to have her husband's will probated when he died some twelve years ago. Other

than that, there was no face-to-face contact. Her will is still here in our files, still valid if there is not one to supersede it. What I was really wondering was if you knew of any attorney she might have used there in Oakman?"

Whether or not Mr. Phillips was trading information, I did not know, but he had given me more in five minutes that I could have hoped for in five years of research. I answered him, "No, I'm afraid my friendship with Mrs. Davis was more business than personal. To tell you the truth, I thought she had always lived in Oakman. I went to see her at the hospital in Springhill the day she died, but I'm afraid she was too incapacitated to say much. She had a very damaging stroke." I could see no reason to reveal the information I had to him. Mr. Phillips was an attorney trying to probate a will, and what I knew of Mrs. Laura Bell Smartt would be of no benefit to that end.

Mr. Phillips asked, "About this letter we received from Oakman telling of Mrs. Davis' death, would you have any idea who sent it?"

"No, I'm afraid not. Have you talked with her housekeeper, Froney Watkins? I believe she and Mrs. Davis were fairly close."

Mr. Phillips answered, "No, as a matter of fact, I have not been able to find a telephone number for her, and I do need to talk to her. Mrs. Davis set up a small pension for Mrs. Watkins some years ago. Do you happen to know how I might contact her?"

I was feeling very guilty now, trying to decide if Mrs. Davis had been dead more than two weeks. That was how long Froney had said she would continue to work. I was feeling even more remorse over the fact that I had not thought to ask once where Mrs. Davis' body might be. I told Mr. Phillips, "I went by the day after Mrs. Davis died and Mrs. Watkins was still working at that time. She informed me that Mr. Davis had paid her for two weeks and she intended to finish out even though Mrs. Davis had died, and I'm sure she will. You might find her at Mrs. Davis' house around eight on Monday morning. Do you have that number?"

Now I was shuffling through papers to see if I had the number before he answered. I found it as Mr. Phillips recited it to me to confirm that her phone number had not changed. Mr. Phillips asked,

"I was wondering, Mr. Wallace, if you might go by and tell Mrs. Watkins to contact me, just in case I don't catch her at the house?"

I would trade that favor for two more questions. "Where will Mrs. Davis be buried, Mr. Phillips?"

He responded, "I'm sorry, I should have told you earlier. I arranged to have her body brought here this past Thursday. She was buried in the city cemetery next to her husband on Friday. She had already made arrangements for this with the Cornerville Funeral Home years ago."

I asked Mr. Phillips, "What will become of her house since there is no family?"

He responded, "She planned for that, too. Her house and her property are to be sold, and the proceeds are to go to the children's home."

After finding out she had grown up there, I had expected no less, even though I did not know her well. I informed Mr. Phillips, "I will be glad to contact Mrs. Watkins for you. If I do not catch her at the house, I'll contact her at home and give her your address."

First, I would need to know where her home was. He recited his office address and phone number to me, thanked me, and hung up the phone. All this information had come easy; I was thankful for that. Mr. Phillips had certainly owed me no explanation. I felt sad about Mrs. Davis' childhood at the orphanage, but it appeared from all indications growing in in an orphanage had not affected her unfavorably. I did find one thing Mr. Phillips said disquieting. He had said there was no family to take Laura when her parents died. That was not true. Sheriff Smartt had told the paper he put Mollie Jean on a train for Nashville on July 4, 1905. He said she was going to his sister's house. That was family, wasn't it? I wondered now what had become of this sister when Laura Belle needed her three years later.

16

THE WEEK AFTER MARY AND I VISITED SOMMERVILLE passed without any added information, except for the revelation of attorney Bill Phillips. I went to work every day watching the clock, waiting for four-thirty to come, and not much more. Work had become more a bother than anything else. I rushed home every day expecting a letter from the Baldwin County Courthouse or the state prison system. The week went by without a response from either.

On Saturday, May 8, I sat with the Reverend Young for two hours or so and brought him up to date. The story of Nathan Sawyer, of course, hit a nerve. He again stated he had learned nothing more than he had already told me. He said he had seen expressions that told him some of the older people knew what he was talking about, but without fail they had offered him no information about Pennsylvania or its past.

Saturday came and, went, again, without a response to our letters. I was beginning to believe there would be none. After all, so many years had passed, Nathan Sawyer was long since dead. I was sure that responding to this request for information was way down on the list of priorities for both the courthouse and the prison system.

Sunday afternoon I lazily thumbed through the journal and came back across a name I had almost forgotten about. Percy Stanley was the deputy that found Harlan Smartt dead. I opened the phone book to see how common the name Stanley was in Oakman, never considering that his name might be there. As I ran my finger down the list of names I was amazed when the name Percy T. Stanley appeared at my fingertip. It had to be a relative, I thought cautiously to myself. He could not possibly still be alive. I thought for one fleeting moment that Mrs. Davis had just died, but then quickly remembered that she was eleven years old when her father died.

Deputy Stanley would have surely been much older.

I dialed the number listed in the phone book, hoping for nothing. It rang several times before an elderly sounding woman answered the phone, very out of breath. "Hello." I asked the woman "Is this the residence of the Percy Stanley who was at one time a deputy here in Oakman?"

She responded, "No, I'm afraid not."

She was poised to say something else, but I interrupted. "Oh, well, thank you anyway."

The woman stated, "this is the residence of Percy Stanley, Jr. whose father was a deputy in Oakman many years go."

I was stunned for a second before I could speak. "May I speak to him please," I asked.

She responded, "Hold the line just a minute." She lay the receiver down without a question as if someone called every day to ask about Deputy Stanley. I did not even know what relationship she was to the man I was about to speak with. She did not say; I assumed she was his wife. I heard the click of another receiver being picked up. The same woman's voice was at the other end, but it was distant. It took a moment or two to understand what she was saying and to realize she was not talking to me.

"Percy, wake up, wake up! You got a phone call. You got to quit falling asleep in this chair. I had to come in from the garden to answer the phone. I can't be out there and in here, too!" If she had mentioned why he had a phone call I had not heard hear.

The man came to the phone and said, "Hello, this is Percy."

"Mr. Stanley, my name is Robert Wallace. I'm doing some research into the Smartt family here in Oakman. I discovered from some old news articles that your father was the one who found Sheriff Smartt dead back in 1908. I was wondering if he ever said anything about that. The old paper didn't have many details."

He asked me, "What was your name again?"

"Robert Wallace," I repeated. I thought he might ask why I wanted to know but didn't.

He responded by stating, "That was before my time, but he told me about them days. That Harlan Smartt wasn't no good. There wasn't a thing to him, my daddy said. Only good thing about him was his wife and those two girls."

I said, "I'm sorry, I don't understand."

He replied, "Well, my daddy said that Harlan Smartt wasn't from around Oakman. He was from somewhere else, can't say as I remember where. Somehow, he married into the Gibbons family; they was pretty well-to-do people around here back then. He married in to them, and that's why he got to be sheriff. His wife's folks put him in that job. My daddy said he was mean to that wife and them girls. Even hit on them sometimes. Just wasn't nothing to him."

I asked him, "Do you happen to recall how he died? The paper just said your father found him dead, didn't say what killed him."

There was the sound of low laughter coming through the phone before he answered. "Now that there was a hell of a thing. My daddy found old Harlan at the bottom of the balcony at the back of the house. He had one boot on, his shirt off, and his pants down around his knees. My daddy always said he believed that Harlan was getting undressed out there on that porch and fell backwards over the rail trying to get his boots off. Broke his neck when he hit the ground. He drank a lot too. My daddy figures he'd had a couple more than usual the night before. He figured he lay there all night. Found an empty bottle up there on the balcony. My daddy always said the devil just got his due; he wasn't no good anyway."

I asked him, "Did your father stay on after that?"

He responded, "No, not for long. The Mayor and that bunch at the city, they thought my daddy knew too much about what went on when Harlan Smartt was sheriff. God rid of him pretty quick. He went back to farming and stayed with it till he died, twenty-five years ago or so."

I asked, "Did he ever say what it was that went on that the Mayor did not want anybody to know about?"

Percy, Jr. responded, "Well sir, my daddy didn't know as much as they thought. Old Smartt hadn't told him much, he wasn't a deputy there but three or four years, and he never did like Sheriff Smartt. I know he didn't like the business with that Colored boy they arrested for raping his daughter. My daddy always thought there was something fishy about that situation, sending him away to be tried and all."

I stated, "That would be Nathan Sawyer. They sent him to Baldwin County to try him."

"Yes, that was it," he answered, with more excitement in his voice, "that was one thing my daddy thought wasn't right. That's where that old Harlan Smartt was from, over there in Baldwin County. I remember that now."

There was a pause in the conversation. Mr. Stanley coughed and then, I believe, spit before he continued. "My daddy never believed that colored boy raped anybody. He believed that Harlan was just sorry enough to use his own daughter to get that boy in trouble."

I asked him, "Get him in trouble for what?"

He responded, "My daddy didn't really know, he just always thought something wasn't right."

I asked, "Was there anything else you might tell me?"

He responded, "No sir; I guess that's about all I remember. Mostly I remember that Harlan Smartt was no good. No good at all."

I thanked Mr. Stanley and hung up the receiver. It was hard to believe that a chance look in the phone book would yield such a fountain of information. As with all the other sources, it was so much information that in itself, led nowhere. Now I was even more anxious to hear from the Baldwin County Courthouse. Deputy Stanley was correct; there certainly was something there that was not right.

Almost a second week had gone by before we heard from the Baldwin County Clerk. It was short, to the point, and disappointing:

Dear Mr. Wallace

In reply to your letter concerning the trial of one Nathan Sawyer in 1905, I'm sorry to inform you that the Baldwin County Courthouse sustained heavy fire damage in 1934. The fire, which began in the records room in the basement, all but destroyed the building and did destroy all trial transcripts on record up until that time. I personally am not familiar with this particular case, but perhaps an area newspaper library would contain the information you need. I'm sorry I cannot assist you further with this matter.

Sincerely,
Ms. Mildred Puckett
District Court Clerk
Baldwin County

I had already seen what newspaper coverage of the story looked like. I wondered for a moment if there was a newspaper in Baldwin County in 1905. Of course, if Harlan Smartt was from Baldwin County as Percy Stanley had said, there was probably very little to be found. It was obvious that the *War and Peace* had found little or a least they did not report it to be public. That for the time-being still left me waiting for an answer from the prison system.

I thought I might drive down to Cornerville and see what information I might find out there. What I really needed to know had happened here in Oakman. Mr. Phillips had told me, I believe, all there was to tell about Mrs. Laura Davis after she left Oakman at age eleven. What I needed to know was still here somewhere.

I came in from work the afternoon of Wednesday, June 8th, to find a note from Mary stating that I had received a call from Mr. James Hard. He requested that I return his call before five that afternoon or after eight the following morning. There was no explanation on the note if he had given any, as to who Mr. Hard was. I dialed the long-distance number, dialing a one, the area code then the number. 205, within the state, but not Oakman. My heart began to pound when the operator at the other end answered the phone.

"Popular Bluff Correctional Facility."

I was stunned for a moment, unable to recall the name of the man I was calling. I had to glance down at the note and locate his name before I could respond. By that time, the operator was repeating her original greeting, a little louder than before.

"Popular Bluff Correctional Facility."

"Mr. James Hard, please."

The operator stated, "that would be Deputy Warden Hard, sir. I'll ring if he's still in."

A second voice answered the phone this time stating, "Warden Hard's office, may I say who's calling?"

I responded, "Bob, I mean Robert Wallace." I was nervous, and I had no idea why. I had done nothing wrong. I think it was that name, Warden Hard. I could imagine what the prisoners called him. The name certainly fit the job.

"Mr. Wallace, this is Deputy Warden Jim Hard. I'm calling to ask you about the letter we received from you about Nathan Sawyer. I wonder if you might give me some idea of exactly what your interest in his case might be?" Again, as with lawyer Phillips, I had to choose my words carefully. Here was someone else who had no need to tell me anything. I was trying to think quickly if there had been another way to approach this, perhaps I should have had Reverend Young field this one for me. It was too late for that now. Warden Hard was on the phone, and I did not want to lose him.

"Well, you see, Mr. Hard, I'm looking into some property here in Oakman that at one time was the Black section of town. The houses burned down there in 1905, and the land has sat idle ever since. I was looking for some old-time residents of Oakman who might know about this area. In doing so, I ran across Nathan Sawyer's name in some old news articles and wondered if he might have some relatives still living in this area. I had not told the whole truth, but I was prepared to do so if I needed to.

"Tell me, Mr. Wallace," stated Warden Hard, "How would information about Nathan or his relatives help you with this matter?"

I responded, "You see, there is some question as to ownership of the land and I'd like to get some information on who actually owned this land before the fire destroyed the houses there." There was a momentary silence. Warden Hard was obviously pondering my question before he gave me an answer.

"To be honest with you Mr. Wallace, I wanted to talk to you

before I released this information to you. The reason I've been so long answering is I took some time to look back over Nathan Sawyer's case before I responded. I wanted to talk to you on the phone to see if I felt like there was any reason to be suspicious of you before I released this information."

"Suspicious?"

"You must understand, Mr. Wallace, that Nathan Sawyer was convicted of raping a white woman in 1905. Ordinarily, a Black man accused of such a crime at that time would have been just hanged or shot, and the people who did it would have felt very few repercussions, if any, from his death. Nathan Sawyer has paid for his crime, and I had no desire to make him pay for it again, especially at this late date. I took some time to check on your background before responding to your request. I could find no information to lead me to believe you intended to do him harm."

Do him harm? My mind was racing. Nathan Sawyer was still alive!

"I also contacted the facility where Nathan Sawyer lives and asked his permission to release this information to you, and he granted it. Why I'm not quite sure."

I was trying to take it all in. Warden Hard had just told me in not so many words that he had checked me out to see if I was a member in good standing of some white supremacist organization that was going to make Nathan Sawyer pay for his crime eighty-three years after the fact. For a moment, I felt angry about his invasion of my privacy, but in retrospect, I should have expected it. After all, so much racism still exists in the world, he had to find out. In an identical situation, I was sure I would have done the same thing. Of course, what really threw me is that up until this moment I thought I was inquiring about the fate of a dead man.

Warden Hard continued without asking me any more questions. The straight-forward, businesslike tone he had disappeared from his voice. There was a slow, almost sorrowful tone to his voice as he told me Nathan's story.

"You see, Mr. Wallace, Nathan Sawyer was here at Poplar Bluff up until 1963. At that time, he had been here fifty-eight years and was seventy-four years old. He was only sixteen years old when he was tried and convicted of rape, just barely sixteen. By the time he left here, he was a trustee of the carpentry shop here at the prison and had been for many years. He was a model prisoner all of his fifty-eight years here. Just like so many other places in the sixties, the prison system was experiencing difficulties. A riot broke out in the prison between the Black and White inmates. During the riot, a group of inmates broke into the carpentry shop, knowing there were many potential weapons there: screwdrivers, chisels, and the like. When they arrived, Nathan had locked all the cabinets that held these tools and refused to tell them where the keys were. A fight broke out, and one of the inmates hit Nathan across the back with a board that had nails driven into the end of it. From all indications, he was hit several times. One of the blows paralyzed him completely from the waist down; another caused partial paralysis of his arms and hands. After a hospital stay of several weeks, he was paroled and moved to a nursing home facility at Greenwood. The prison had no facilities for an inmate in his condition. Even if he hadn't received significant injury, he had attempted to keep the inmates out of the shop, he had been here fifty-eight years, and he was seventy-four years old. The parole was well-deserved. It's a shame it had to be a release to a nursing home bed."

I questioned the warden, "How old is Mr. Sawyer now?" I felt Warden Hard would know without my subtracting the time.

He responded, "Well, as a matter of fact, he is ninety-nine years old now. The nursing home tells me he is in perfect health other than his original paralysis, which has improved only slightly." Before I could ask, Warden Hard answered my next question, he continued, "And they tell me his mind is perfect, sharp as a tack."

I asked the warden, "When may I see Mr. Sawyer, and what did you say is the name of the nursing home?"

He responded, "You will have to arrange the day and time with the nursing home. The facility is called Greenwood Manor and is on Highway 69 in Greenwood. You will have to get the exact location from them. I would appreciate it if you would give me a call when you arrange your visit."

I thought one more question would not hurt since Warden Hard had 'checked me out." I asked him, "Warden Hard, do you know if Mr. Sawyer ever said he was innocent or guilty?"

Warden Hard answered, "I suspect he was afraid to say much of anything when he got here, but years later he said he was innocent. Of course, 90 percent of the inmates say they're innocent. Most likely a few are." He answered me without committing. I suspected that was the best he could do, considering his position.

I thanked Warden Hard and assured him I would call when I made my plans. I was certain he was going to make some kind of provisions for Nathan Sawyer's safety, however, small. Since my interest in him was purely to talk, I had no reservations about informing the warden of my visit. In a strange sort of way, I was glad he had shown such an interest in Nathan Sawyer's well-being.

I hung up the phone and for a few minutes thought about that name again and how well it fit the bill. The inmates most assuredly called him 'Warden Hardass,' what else could they do? I tried to imagine for a moment what he might look like and wondered if any of them called him 'hardass' to his face. I had to get the thought out of my mind before I called back so I would not mistakenly ask for Deputy Warden "Hardass". I felt like I might laugh when I thought about it to myself. *"Popular Bluff Correctional Facility." "Could I speak with Warden Hardass please?"*

June 8, 1988 (Wednesday): Talked with Warden Hard at Popular Bluff. Nathan Sawyer still alive. Lives at Greenwood Manor Nursing Home. 99 years old. Need to find out when I can see him. Maybe he has the truth….

I called Greenwood Manor that night and inquired about visiting hours. I inquired further into when was the best time to visit Nathan Sawyer. Visiting hours, the nurse that answered the phone informed me, were from ten in the morning until eight at night. She suggested that perhaps the best time for Nathan would be after lunch, perhaps one-thirty or two.

I planned my visit for two o-clock the afternoon of June 11th. I informed Warden Hard of my plans Thursday afternoon and asked if he had any objections to the Reverend Young coming with me. I was not really sure why I was asking permission to bring the Reverend or informing the warden as to when I intended to visit. Nathan Sawyer was a free man, paroled twenty-five years ago. But I had agreed to these conditions and still respected Warden Hard's concern over my interest in this ninety-nine-year-old man.

After talking with the warden, I went by Reverend Young's church to try to catch him and see if he wanted to ride to Greenwood with me. I knew, almost without asking, that he would. I believed from looking at a map that it was about one hundred fifty miles south of Oakman, very near Poplar Bluff. A three-hour trip, maybe a little longer. The nursing home, I had been told when I called, was on this side of Greenwood. Right on the highway as you enter town, couldn't miss it.

The Reverend Young and I drove into the parking lot of Greenwood Manor at 1:50 p.m. Saturday afternoon. I had brought him up-to-date on the trip down. I really do not know how I expected Greenwood to look. I guess I had given it very little thought. It was a long building that really looked more like a house than a nursing home. There were large double glass doors under a large porch in the middle of the building. On either side there was a multitude of individual windows that ran the length of the building. In front of the porch was a sign marked 'Visitor Parking.' We parked the car and went under the large gabled roof. The front office and receptionist were to the left, right inside the door. The office was enclosed in a glass that looked out into the hall as well as out on the large front porch.

"May I help you please?" The woman behind the glass sat in a rolling chair with a headset on that was no doubt for answering the phone. She was small and frail, and really, at a glance, appeared unhealthy.

"Yes," I responded, "Could you direct us to Mr. Nathan Sawyer's room?"

She rolled the chair in which she was sitting over to the window that looked out on the porch and strained to look down the right-hand side and said, "Nathan is sitting out there on the porch, at the far end. You walked by him on the way in." There was a look of excitement on her face when she turned back around, as if she had forgotten something. "You'll have to excuse me; I have an errand to run. Go out on the porch. He will be glad to see you."

She was taking the headset off and moving out the door that entered the hall as she spoke.

Reverend Young and I moved back onto the porch and walked cautiously toward the elderly Black gentleman whose wheelchair was parked at the other end. His head was thrown back as if he might be asleep.

"Mr. Sawyer, I'm Robert Wallace. Warden Hard told you I was asking about you."

He slowly brought his head forward and looked as if he might be having to focus his eyes to see. I did not know what a hundred years old looked like, but I didn't think it looked like this. He was a stately looking gentleman that I could see was tall even though he was sitting. His hair was yellow-grey and his skin very black, but I could find very few of the lines in his face that I thought came with that much age.

I continued, "this is a friend of mine, Reverend Nathan Young. We are both from Oakman. We would like to ask you a few questions if we might?"

As he extended a hand I could see where he had aged. His massive fingers felt like coarse rope when I grasped his hand. The veins in his hand twisted and stood out like they might rupture at any moment. As he shook our hands, a State Trooper's car drove into the parking lot. A young man entered the building through the front doors as we had earlier, tipping his hat as he went in the door. I imagined this was what the operator had forgotten, and this was Nathan Sawyer's protection, arranged by Warden Hard just in case I was not what I had represented myself to be. The trooper had gone into the office and had taken a seat at the window. I could see more of his reflection in the window than his body. I could tell from the reflection that he was straining to look toward us. Nathan Sawyer turned our hands loose, motioned for us to sit in the rocking chairs directly in front of him, and spoke for the first time.

"What can I do for you gentlemen?"

Reverend Young and I had decided on the way down that I would ask the questions as long as Nathan answered. If he seemed uncomfortable with me, Reverend Young would take over the conversation.

"I was wondering," I asked him, "If you might tell us about what happened there in Oakman, in 1905, with the Smartt girl?" He did not ask why I wanted to know. That was good, because I was not sure I had an answer.

"Well sir, you want me to tell you all of it from the start?"

"If you don't mind talking about it."

He moved his buttocks from side to side in his chair before he began. "I don't know what happened to Miss Mollie Jean. Whatever happened, I didn't do it. My daddy and me been working around the Smartt place that December. My daddy was a carpenter, unusual for a Colored man back then, but he had learned from his father. Well, sir, we was over putting some shingles on the roof, fixing some porch boards. Just doing some little jobs around the house, been working several days. Miss Mollie Jean would come out and talk, bring us water, and like that. One day she was standing on the back porch talking to me while I pitched cedar shakes up the roof to my daddy."

He sighed and moved in his chair again before he continued.

"I don't even know where Sheriff Smartt came from, out the back door or around the house or where. He was just there all at once. He had that Miss Mollie by the hair of the head, dragging her in the back door of the house cussing her all the way. When he got her in the house he be slapping her, and she was crying, but not hollering out loud. I couldn't hear every word, but most of it. He says that she was trash just like her momma. He says she loved niggers too and she was just like her. He says he's going to beat nigger-loving out of her before it's too late. Now sir, the next thing he's out in the yard and got me by the collar and shaking me while my daddy coming down the ladder. He axed who in the hell I think I am out on the back porch talking to his daughter. He says he'll kill me if he ever sees me around his daughter again. Then he slings me over towards my daddy and tells him to take my nigger ass back to Pennsylvania where I belong, before I get in more trouble than I can get out of. He hollered at my daddy as we went round the side of the house for him to get me home and bring his ass back and finish that roof. Then he told him he better not ever bring my black ass with him again. Me and my daddy got back in the wagon and he rode down the street and told me to go home and stay in the rest of the day. He told me not to pay no attention to Harlan Smartt. He says he knows I wasn't doing nothing or planning on doing nothing with Miss Mollie. He says that Sheriff Smartt is crazy, and I better stay away from there for me and Miss Mollie's sake. I went on home and didn't go out of the house for two or three days. My daddy didn't say no more about Sheriff Smartt until that February."

He stopped for a moment and adjusted in his chair again before he continued on. Time had certainly not affected his memory or his wind. He had wanted to tell this story to an attentive audience for a very long time.

"Well sir," he began, "that February was the first time I heard anything about Sheriff Smartt again. My daddy came in one day and told me the sheriff wanted me to come over and split stove wood for him. Says he sorry about the way he treated me, that he knows I wasn't doing nothing with Miss Mollie. So, my daddy tells me to go that next morning and split that stove wood and Sheriff Smartt will pay me when I'm through. My daddy tells me that if Mollie Jean comes out for me to leave and not look back. So, I went that Saturday morning about seven. My daddy told me not to go too early 'cause I'll wake them up. Well sir, I was splitting and stacking that wood right smart, about an hour or so. All of a sudden there was terrible screaming up there at that porch. I was up my daddy's ladder he had left and on that porch like I had wings. The doors up there was open and Miss Mollie was laying there on the bed. She was beat up and bleeding some terrible. I believes her hands were tied to the bedpost and her night clothes was all torn up. She was showing everywhere, I moved on off that porch to the bed, put the covers up over what was showing that wasn't 'sposed to, and started to untie her and the next thing I know somebody knocked me over the head, and I was bleeding and then I was sleeping." He bowed his head as if might not continue.

I asked him, "Do you remember what happened next?"

He answered, "Never forget it sir, never. I woke up hog-tied in the back of Sheriff Smartt's wagon. He stopped and rolled me out in the street in front of the jail. Told his deputy to drag me into the cell and lock me up 'fore he killed me. He tell that deputy that he just found me in his house having his daughter. He says I tied her up and beat her to make her do it. Well sir, don't remember nothing happen for a few days. Then two sheriffs come and put me in shackles and chains and puts me in a wagon and says they taking me to Baldwin County to stand trial. Says old Sheriff Smartt wants my rights protected and they laugh about that."

Again, he stopped as if he might not continue. Maybe he just needed time to breathe. He was ninety-nine years old, after all. I asked him, "What happened in Baldwin County?"

He responded, "Well sir, nothing happened 'til May. Then this white man who say he was my lawyer came round and says he goin to defend me. He says it be best if I don't say nothing to nobody. I told him I didn't do nothing to Miss Mollie Jean. That I was trying to help her. He tells me I better not say nothing. So, I didn't say nothing. Next thing I know we's in the court in front of the jury. Sheriff Smartt say he find me up in Miss Mollie's room raping her. That I put a ladder up there and climbed up and beat her up and raped her."

I asked him, "Did Miss Mollie come tell her side?"

"No sir," he responded, "The judge he read a letter from Miss Mollie saying I did what her father say I did and that she was too young and too sick to have to come tell a humi...hum.."

I filled in stating, "Humiliating?"

He responded, "Yes sir, humil-ating story like that in public. Judge says she don't have to come tell that story in front of all these peoples just 'cause this Colored boy here don't know how to act. Judge says I'm going to Poplar Bluff for the rest of my life. They took me down there the next day and in 1963 I came here."

I asked him, "Who else testified besides Sheriff Smartt?"

He responded, "Nobody, just him."

Reverend Young and I turned to look at one another to find we both had red eyes. I shivered at the thought of such a trial even in 1905. I asked Nathan, "Did you ever hear from your family again?"

He responded, "One time, after I had been at Poplar Bluff for about a year, my sister Nellie come to see me. She said Pennsylvania done burned while I was gone, and that Sheriff Smartt done told them not to think about me no more or they'd be in trouble just like me. She says they know I didn't do nothing, but they didn't know how to help me. Nellie wrote me when my father died in 1925. Then she wrote me when my mother died in 1933. She had married and moved to Chicago before either one of them died and I stopped hearing from her in about 1940 or 41. I guess Nellie dead, too. I guess I outlived them all, but I wish sometimes I had died when they did, 'cause I sure didn't have no life. Nobody ever axed me how old I was, but I turned sixteen while I was there in the Baldwin County Jail. No sir, wasn't much of a life."

I sat in the rocking chair across from Nathan Sawyer wondering what I might say to ease his pain and mine. I was feeling sick at my stomach as I thought about his wasted life. I looked over my shoulder and could still see the trooper's reflection in the office window. I was at a complete loss for any words that would help. Now I knew why I had brought Reverend Young with me.

For the first time since our introduction he spoke to Nathan. "I'm truly sorry for your long suffering, brother Nathan, but the Lord knows you were innocent of the crime for which you were sentenced. I am sure he has prepared a special place for you that is like no other in Heaven. Is there anything we can do for you before we go?"

Nathan responded, "No sir, Reverend, I reckon not. You come

back and visit when you get a chance. Talk about something else. I ain't never told that story to no one and don't really care nothin' about telling it again."

"We understand, of course, brother Nathan."

Reverend Young stood up and I followed his cue. We shook Nathan Sawyer's twisted hands once more and wished him well. I felt certain that I would not see him again. I was ashamed to admit to myself that what had happened to him sickened me so that I would be unable to visit him again. As we backed out of the parking lot, I could see the trooper was on the office phone. No doubt he had been told to report in to someone when we left. He could report that Nathan Sawyer had not been hurt, at least not by us. His hurt had begun eighty-five years ago and festered right up until now. There was probably little or nothing I could do for Nathan Sawyer now, but I was more determined than ever to find out what happened there in Pennsylvania on that July night in 1905. Nathan Sawyer was at Poplar Bluff by then, but whoever hid the brooch in the fireplace, I was sure, had seen everything. I was hoping that someone else was still alive, too.

17

ON SUNDAY MORNING, I SAT ACROSS FROM MARY AT
the kitchen table and tried to see where I was in my search for the
truth. I looked back through the journal to see if there was something
I missed. On a separate sheet of paper, I went back over my entries
and made short notes to bring me up-to-date.

March 25 (Fri) – Tommy brought me the brooch
March 26 (Sat) – Went to Oppenheim Jewelry
March 28 (Mon) – Talked with Mr. Humphries, told me Penn
Road used to be the Black Section of town.
April 11 (Mon) – City maps, Pennsylvania disappeared in
1905. Thomas Stanley, then William Bell were surveyors.
Notation about Federal protection.
April 16 (Sat) – Saw Lazarus Cemetery for the first time. Met
Reverend Young for the first time. Pennsylvania and cemetery
directly in line.
May 2 (Sat) – Met Mrs. Laura Bell Davis for first time. Said
fire in Pennsylvania was accident. Told me about Daniel
Brewer and Federal protection.
May 7 (Sat) - Went in Lazarus Cemetery with Reverend
Young. 9 bodies buried together. Mother and child buried at
tree. Date of these 11 deaths 07/05/05.
May 9 (Mon) – Met Froney Watkins, tells of Mrs. Davis'
hospitalization on 5/1. Then to Springhill on 5/7. Talked with
Caroline Kelly, ICU nurse, same day.
May 22 (Sun) – Lawyer Phillips called – Told me about Mr.
Davis' childhood. Moved back to Oakman around age 60.
Froney's pension. Buried in Cornerville 5/18, city cemetery

next to husband Gerald. Info. About death from anonymous source in Oakman.

May 29 (Sun) – Talked with Percy Stanley, Jr. – Harlan Smartt died in fall from balcony, broken neck, probably drunk, Married a Gibbons woman – Laura and Mollie's mother. June 4 (Sat) - Heard from Baldwin Co. Court Clerk – fire in 1938. No court record for Nathan's trial.

June 8 (Wed) – Warden Hard contacted. Nathan Sawyer still alive.

June 11 (Sat) – Reverend Young and I visited Nathan at Greenwood Manor Nursing Home. 99 years old. Told story – says he was innocent. Only Sheriff Smartt testified at trial. Statement from Mollie Jean read in court.

I wondered what, or who, the key was. I had traveled from a brooch and gloves hidden in a fireplace to a ninety-nine-year-old man who was sentenced to life for a crime he most likely did not commit. Neither appeared to have anything to do with the other. Nathan had gone to prison before Pennsylvania burned and its people migrated to the river. He wasn't there the night the brooch was hidden in the fireplace. He was by then sitting in a cell at Poplar Bluff. Laura Bell Smartt was a child of eight years old. Even if she had found the truth in adulthood, she had taken it with her to grave leaving me only two names with which to find it.

I looked over the notes trying to find something or someone I missed. I wondered if Mrs. Davis had given me everything she had intended to in her weakened state. If she did, it was not enough. I had all but forgotten about Tommy and Jack Morrow. I had almost forgotten how much easier it was just to dig something out of the ground and put it in the garage, never knowing or caring whether or not there is a story to go with it. I wished somewhere deep in myself that Tommy had not brought the brooch to me in the first place. Then there would have been no reason to pursue its owner, which I had not yet found. I had discovered something that I could have gone a lifetime without knowing, but it was too late for that now, too.

As I turned through the journal and made short notes, I discovered something I had not seen before. Mary had retrieved the ad from the newspaper that University Hospital had placed for information about Mrs. Davis. This was the ad that had alerted someone, some anonymous someone in Oakman to contact Mr. Phillips about her death. That person was undoubtedly the missing piece to the puzzle, Someone, who knew enough to contact a lawyer that no one else knew existed. He or she was probably the key that turned the lock, but I had no way to find them.

Mary had cut the ad out and carefully taped it to the top of the last page I had made entries on:

Wanted:

Information

about the late

Mrs. Laura Bell

Davis. Call collect

897-5656,

ex. 4075

That simple ad had alerted the person to contact Mr. Phillips and let him know that the hospital was looking for someone to finalize Mrs. Davis' death and pay her bill.

As I stared at the ad, an avenue of information came to me that I had not considered before. Perhaps, this was the way to find the missing link. Maybe there was a chance that the person who hid the brooch and gloves in the fireplace so long ago read the paper now. Time, of course, was not on my side. How many Nathan Sawyers could possibly still be alive to tell their story. I desperately hoped someone knew this story and was still alive to tell it.

I turned to the empty pages at the back of the journal and composed an ad that would mean nothing to anyone but me and someone who knew about the brooch and gloves hidden in the fireplace in Pennsylvania.

Wanted:

Information

about an old

cameo brooch
found in
Pennsylvania.

Mary went Monday morning and rented a post office box. Six months was the minimum time she could rent it. Hopefully, it would not take that long. She then placed the ad in the paper. The clerk in the want-ads section of *The Sentinel* stared but did not comment as she placed the ad and collected the money.

Monday afternoon was the next time I heard from or saw Tommy, and Jack was with him. As I sat in the kitchen, there was the obvious sound of two men fighting out in the street in front of the house. I went on the front porch to discover Jack coming toward the front door, cussing, and Tommy attempting to stop him without success. Jack came up on the front porch and began cussing. He positioned himself about six inches from my face.

Jack addressed me asking, "I want to know what the hell you know about this business out on Penn Road? I lost a lot of damn business out there and want to know what in the hell your ass has got to do with it?"

I stood motionless for a moment not knowing how to answer. Jack was mad, that was for sure, not that he had to be mad to cuss. His face was red and his lips white. He made a fist with his right hand. I readied myself to block it, and swing if I had to. He stepped back an inch or two before he spoke again. It was not until then that I could smell the alcohol on his breath. Tommy stood at his back, like me, readying himself to hold Jack back if need be. Jack continued his tirade.

"Something happened out there. The city won't budge on this and I got a lot of money and men ready to go! I'm losing money every day out there and you got something to do with it, by God, and I want to know what!" His fist had unclenched, but his lips remained white, and there was a fire in his eyes I had not seen when he first came on the porch.

I finally spoke, "Honestly, Jack, I don't know what you're talking about. I have nothing to do with the city's stopping work on Penn

120

Road. What makes you think I do?"

Jack responded, "Because, you were the last to see those city maps that showed when the city bought that land. You signed out for it last. The damn book's been gone ever since. The mayor has refused to talk to me ever since. All I get is some damn run around, city's got financial trouble. They had plenty of money until you looked at that map. What the hell was on that damn map?"

I answered, "In 1905, nothing was on it."

"What do you mean 'nothing in 1905'? There's nothing on the son of a bitching land now! Never has been. Now what in the hell is going on?"

Tommy continued to stand cautiously behind his back without speaking as I answered Jack.

"That used to be the Black section of town. The houses burned in 1905 and they moved down to the river. That's all the maps I looked at showed. It was there and then in 1905 it was gone. The map said the city acquired the land that year, nothing more than that."

"Acquired, what the hell does that mean? Who did they buy the land from? Who did the map say the damn land was bought from?"

I responded, "It didn't. I'm telling you it just said 'acquired'."

Jack asked, "Whose name was on the damn deed? Who sold the land?"

I told him, "I didn't look for the deed. Just the map. The only name on it was the surveyor, Bell, William Bell, I think."

Jack then asked me, "Bell, like mayor Bell?"

That connection, if there was one, had never occurred to me. I looked over Jack's shoulder as I thought about it. He had finally grown tired of trying to get information I didn't have. He turned and descended the front steps back to his truck. It had been parked idling on the street with the engine running and the door open the whole time he had been cussing me. Tommy trailed behind trying to convince Jack to let him drive. The last thing I heard Jack say was for Tommy to get his 'buddy,' Wallace to take him home. Jack slammed the door almost catching Tommy's hand in it and sped away. Tommy stood for a few minutes looking down at the sidewalk shuffling his feet before he turned and walked back toward the porch with his head down. Tommy came up on the porch and sat, continuing to hold his head down. I sat across from him and waited for him to talk first.

He began, "I'm really sorry, Mr. Wallace. My dad is really upset. He really has lost a lot of money on that city job. He was just looking for somebody to blame. You were the only one he could think of tonight. He's been trying to get some commercial work for years, then when he finally did they pulled it from him before he could even get started. I'm really sorry."

I was only half listening to Tommy and half thinking about what Jack had said; Mayor Bell, William Bell. It was just too farfetched. William Bell had done the city survey in 1905, the year the city had 'acquired' Pennsylvania. Before that, the survey had been done by Stanley… Thomas Stanley. Then there was the deed that I had never thought about looking for. There would be a record of that transaction too, if it were legal. Tommy's head was still bowed, and I had to say something that would comfort him.

"Don't worry about it, Tommy. Your dad's having a bad time of it. He needed to lash out. We all feel that way sometimes. I've got an idea, though, about how we can help him and convince him that I had nothing to do with the city pulling his contracts."

Tommy held his head erect for the first time since his father sped away down the street. He still was not smiling but at least he was looking and listening to what I had to say.

"Do you know what to ask for at the courthouse to find out about the land on Penn Road in 1905, who bought it and who sold it?"

Tommy replied, "Sure. We need to go the Probate Office, but we need a month to go with the year, or it might take a long time to find. Of course, a name wouldn't hurt either. The name of who bought or who sold the land. That would be a big help."

I responded, "September 1905, is the month and the year we are looking for. The name I am not so sure of, maybe Brewer. That we'll

122

just have to search out. Maybe we can turn something up."

I invited Tommy in and told him to stay for supper. By the time Tommy had eaten, Mary had asked him to stay the night, hoping it might ease his mind if he didn't have to see his father until he was sober again. Tommy declined and timidly asked for a ride home. I drove him home and waited while he ascended the stairs to the apartment over his parents' garage. He had agreed to meet me at the courthouse in the morning and help me go through the records. I drove home wondering if there was anything to find there. Apparently, someone had made the city map for that year unavailable, too. I was hoping whoever it was had not thought of that. As with everything that had to do with this story, anything was possible. I had nothing to do for the time being but wait to see if I would hear from the ad. The ad would run for one week, from Tuesday until Monday of next week. Until then I would just have to wait.

Tommy was waiting for me at seven-thirty the next morning in the coffee shop on the first floor of the courthouse. As we sat waiting for the Probate Office to open, I told him the story up until now. From his bringing me the brooch right up to Nathan Sawyer. I held back for the time-being, the part about the ad, which had started today. I was not really sure why I told him everything, but I felt certain he needed something to help take his mind off his troubles. He appeared to listen with great interest as I talked, only occasionally commenting.

I felt, as I told the story, like I had when he and Bobby were boys. There was a genuine look of excitement in his face just as there had been when he dug indistinguishable objects out of the ground as a boy. I felt guilty that I had not included him in the search from the beginning. Now he had heard the whole story and perhaps this was a better time. He didn't mention Jack, and in a way, I was glad that, for the time-being, he had separated himself from his father's smothering hold. I thought once I might jokingly ask him how he had gotten out of work today, but I could find no good reason to remind him he had stepped across his father's imaginary line.

The Probate Office opened about 8:05. The clerk opened the door and put down a rubber stop to hold it back. We entered and stood at the desk waiting for her to return from the shelves. When she did, Tommy did the talking.

"We'd like to see the transfer of deeds for September 1905."

Without a word she turned and walked along a row of shelves and around behind them out of sight. A light came on the phone at the clerks' desk as we waited and went out a few minutes before she returned. She placed a leather-bound book on the desk in front of us. It was perhaps just half the size and weight of the books that contained the city maps. On the binder of the book was: *September 1905.*

The clerk informed us, "Just take it there to the table and if you need any others, I'll be glad to get them for you. Please be careful not to make any marks in it."

I was not absolutely sure, but I believed as she sat back down that this was the clerk that had let me out of the records cage downstairs. Tommy and I sat down at the table side-by-side and started turning pages at the beginning. The transactions were listed in alphabetical order, using the seller's name. Each transaction was described using the same method as on the maps. Section, township, range, etc. I had copied down this information and brought it with me, but for the time being we were looking more for a name. What name I was not sure, but I would know it when I found it.

I took the card on which I had written the land description and started down the pages. As I read, Tommy turned the page when I got to the bottom. The listings were fairly simple, just as the city maps had been. I began reading: 'September 3, 1905. Charles A. Swift conveyed to Rupert O. Cain 7 acres more or less described as follows.' Then there would be a description of the land giving, section, township, and range. Then came a description of specific boundaries: A line running 1500 feet northwest to a line running 1120 feet south, etc. I was looking intently at names and not land, since I was afraid I would not be able to spot the description of Pennsylvania anyway.

After running down the pages carefully for perhaps eight or ten minutes, what I had been looking for came into view on September 17, 1905. On that date, Harlan Smartt conveyed from his daughter, Mollie Jean, whose whereabout are unknown, and Laura Belle, who is a minor, land inherited from their mother, Ruth Lorena Smartt, to the city of Oakman, land described below: From the north east quarter of the north west quarter of section 14, township 10, range 7 containing 23 acres more or less.

How convenient for everybody! The sheriff had sold to the city in the absence of his dead wife, land that actually belonged to his daughter. Land that not two months before had been occupied by better than two hundred people. People whose homes had burned to the ground in a questionable fire. A fire that had not burned ten or twenty of their homes to the ground but every single one. Deputy Stanley had said it best, "Something wasn't right." Indeed, something was as rotten as it could be.

My mind was reeling as I copied down the text from the book. I wondered now how much Mrs. Davis had really known about Pennsylvania that she didn't tell me. Her mother had somehow ended up with the land that she had told me belonged to Daniel Brewer. Land she had told me was occupied by Black people since before the Civil War. How had her mother ended up with it? I suspected, too, that the city had discovered they might not own it either, and that was the holdup with the library Jack Morrow was supposed to have started months ago. The city had, no doubt, left the land idle for eighty-three years, waiting for its' long-lost owner to show up, or waiting for long-lost relatives to die out. I wondered now if mayor after mayor had discovered this information and, not known what to do with it, did nothing. Mayor Bell thought it was over, the secret was finely safe. He had given a contract to Jack Morrow to build on it. The surveyors had been there over six months ago. That undoubtedly was when the city attorney or someone informed mayor Bell that the city might not own this tract of land. The truth was it may belong to some Black men or women now squeezed together down by the river. The mayor had probably wished by now his term would end before someone asked him why the new library was not under construction as he had promised. The 1905 map book, no wonder Jack couldn't find it. Someone was probably instructed to throw it off the river bridge in the middle of the night.

This one entry had, like so many other revelations, opened a whole new set of doors. Like the others, I had found the key, and perhaps this one might turn the lock. Tommy looked at me strangely as I wildly wrote down the information from the ledger. He had not understood what we found, and I chose not to explain it to him in the courthouse. I laid the book on the counter for the clerk to return it to the shelves. I felt certain that if we asked for it tomorrow it would be lost like the 1905 map book.

I hurried Tommy out of the courthouse and did not begin to explain until we were across the street. I stopped talking twice to allow passers-by to get to the other side of the street, not knowing whether or not they were city employees. Tommy was elated to have something to tell his father. I was not sure that was such a good idea. Jack Morrow was a little like Harlan Smartt.

Telling him he had lost the contract because the city didn't really own the land was one thing. Telling him the land belonged to some Black man down on the river was quite another matter entirely.

18

I WENT HOME WITH NO RECOLLECTION OF WHETHER I had called in late for work. Those feelings of being consumed that **had** overcome me before, had taken hold again. I did not recall because I did not care. I wanted an answer to all these questions and I wanted it now. My world was fast becoming of no importance to me. What had happened there in Pennsylvania before and after July 5, 1905, was all that was important for me to know. Now, more than ever I needed the truth.

I went and planted myself on the couch and could barely hear Mary calling and making my excuses. I think she had said she didn't know when I would be back to work, which for the time being was the best answer to give. I lay on the couch trying to decide what to do next with this newly discovered information. I imagined to myself that I might just go to Mayor Bell and present him with what I knew, but then I had no way to be absolutely sure if he would, or could, do anything about it. He was, no doubt, just as perplexed as I was. Then I thought about going to the next city council meeting and bringing it up in session for all to question. Again, I could see no gain to that. If Tommy had taken this information straight to Jack, Mayor Bell was undoubtedly due for a long question and answer period any minute. There was always the paper, the *Oakman Sentinel.* I could always sic a reporter on the information and let him present it to the people. Then, again, this was bad news and there was no way to know if the paper would really report it the way it was.

After a long session with myself, I decided the best thing to do was give this one to Reverend Young, let him field this one. The information I had obtained had to do with injustice; that was something he would probably be better equipped to pursue.

Selfishness also dictated that this was truly not my fight anyway, it belonged to Reverend Young and the Black population of Oakman. I was wrong, of course; it was my fight, too, if there was any decency at all left in my life. I had spent my entire life isolated from injustice. I was white and could not possibly feel the pain of these people when the white population in Oakman took away what was rightfully theirs and pushed them to the river. I very much hoped that only a few people were involved in the fire in Pennsylvania on that July night, but I feared there were many. I also hoped to myself that only Harlan Smartt was involved in taking away the land, but again I doubted he had acted alone.

I told Mary I was going to see Reverend Young and give him what I had, suggesting that perhaps now was the time to call in a lawyer and see just exactly what had transpired. Even if these questions could be answered, they would not answer the old ones. For myself, I still needed to know who had owned the brooch and what had been her fate. I went to Reverend Young's church there on Wheeler Street and found him out in the front doing his gardening in a flower bed. We sat on the steps first, and then entered the church and I went back over the city records to him, re-emphasizing what we already knew about Daniel Brewer and his promise one hundred fifty years ago.

"Mr. Wallace," began Reverend Young, "if what you believe to be true is true, why would you bring it to light? Why would you hold these people to be judged for all to see?"

I responded, "Reverend Young, if what I think happened in 1905 did in fact, happen then it was wrong. If the city continues to cover it up until this day, then they are even more wrong now. The color of the people affected by these lies is of no consequence. What is going on here is wrong regardless of the color of the people that it was, and is, happening to. I'm not a martyr, Reverend Young, and do not profess to be, but I know the difference between right and wrong."

The Reverend Young and I talked for a while longer and I told him about the ad I had placed in the paper. I assured him that if

Stephen D. Graham | The Lazarus Tree

additional information came to light because of the ad, I would be sure and pass it on. He thanked me for passing this much on and assured me that he would use it cautiously.

I drove back home feeling relieved that I had turned over this secret to someone else. I knew Reverend Young would use it to help heal old wounds rather than open new ones. I had done little to help Jack and Tommy's situation, but perhaps just having the truth would help them, too.

My ad had come out in today's paper. I hoped as I drove along the river that there was someone left in Oakman that had all the answers I needed. I could only pray they saw the ad. The week passed without an answer to my ad. Mary or I one went every day to the post office to check the box, only to find a lot of junk addressed to our box rather than our name. Jack and Tommy came by once and I tried to explain to Jack that I believed the city did not own the land, without revealing to him who I thought did. He was sober this time and apologized for the scene on the front porch earlier in the week. Other than that, there was very little to tell. Reverend Young and Oakman's first (and only) Black attorney were pursuing Mayor Bell and the deed to Pennsylvania. I did nothing more than wait for the mail at the post office hoping for an answer to the ad.

The week passed, as did the weekend, without an answer. Finally, on Wednesday, June 2, there was a hand-written card placed in the box alongside the junk mail. It was hard to read, obviously written by someone who was fast losing control over his or her hand. The ink on the card looked as if it might still be wet and was smudged in a few places. On the card was a simple message to let me know whoever the anonymous author was, that he or she knew what I wanted to know. The card instructed me to come to the Lazarus Church on Friday, the 24th, but there was no time. Whether or not that was intentional, I had no way of knowing.

Both Wednesday and Thursday night had been sleepless ones waiting for Friday morning to come. I was at Lazarus Church at six-thirty in the morning. It was not until I parked that I wondered if I might have to wake Reverend Young to let me in. I never noticed whether or not the doors were locked. When I tried them, it was apparent to me that they had never been equipped with locks. I entered, closing the door behind me, and took a seat on the front pew that Reverend Young and I had sat in before, I sat, paced, and occasionally stared out the window at the Lazarus Tree waiting from whomever had answered my ad.

Three hours had passed before I heard the doors open again and I was most surprised to see Froney Watkins and a young woman who very much favored her bringing the doors back. There was also a look of surprise on her face, but neither she nor the woman with her commented. They ascended the two steps that entered the church and for the first time I saw a third woman with them and who was walking between them. They helped her to the top step and as she entered the church, they closed the doors behind her. She moved up the aisle toward me with somewhat awkward but very deliberate steps. She walked with a cane that placed heavy on the floor with her left foot as she came up the aisle. She was old, very old, there was no doubt about this. The closer she came, the more of her age I could see. Her face and hands were full of the lines time had left. One eye appeared hazed over by a cataract. I thought she might lose the reading glasses perched on her nose every time her cane hit the floor. As she neared the front of the church, I could see she had rolled her stockings down to keep them in place as her printed dress swayed with her awkward movement. The dress buttoned up the front and she had missed a buttonhole, making the dress hang very uneven on her body.

As she turned to come around in front of the pew I was sitting in, I stood up wondering if I should have offered to help her come this far. I noticed for the first time as she sat down that she was clutching a purse close to her body. There was a newspaper protruding from the top not allowing it to close. I could see the date across the top: 'Sunday, June 17, 1988.' Once she had taken her seat, she motioned for me to sit beside her as she fumbled for something in her purse. She spoke for the first time after findings the

130

handkerchief she had been searching for. I noticed as she wiped her brow that she was wearing a very old wig. It was silver grey and the material to which the hair was attached showed through when the light hit it a certain way. She let me know she was the person I needed to talk to with her opening statement.

"I always wondered when somebody goin' to find Miz Ruthie's brooch and gloves out there in that old fireplace in Pennsylvania. Thought I might die before they was found"

I had not mentioned the gloves or the fireplace in the ad. This was definitely the person I had been looking for!

She continued, "So you want to know about that brooch and them gloves, why they was there, and who they belonged to?"

I responded, "I want to know all you can tell me about Pennsylvania and the people who lived there, Mrs. -?"

"Mrs. Annie May Watkins. Why should I tell you what I know about Pennsylvania?"

I had to think a moment before I answered. She was fishing for ulterior motives before she gave me anything. I had to give her the right answer, even though I was not really sure what it might be. I answered her question stating, "because I'm the only one who ever cared enough to ask."

She stared at the cross at the front of the church, and a tear rolled down one of the deep lines in her face. She nodded her head and wiped her check with the handkerchief she had taken from her purse before she spoke. "I don't believe I caught your name."

I responded, "Robert Wallace."

Mrs. Watkins asked me, "Did you bring Miz Ruthie's brooch with you?" I reached in my pocket and brought out the brooch still in the velvet box Mary had put it in six months ago. I had been carrying it in my pocket again since the ad came out in the paper. She took the brooch from me and opened the box, looking in it without touching the brooch. Both of her eyes were beginning to become red, but there were no tears on her cheeks. She handed back the brooch before speaking again.

"Where would you like me to start, Mr. Robert Wallace?"

"Can you tell me anything about Daniel Brewer? Can you go back that far?"

She laughed a low, graveled laugh before she answered. "Now, Mr. Wallace, I'm old, 108 years, but I'm not that old. I can tell you what I been told about Daniel Brewer, but I don't know it for sure."

"Anything you have to say will be of great interest to me, Mrs. Watkins."

"Please call me Annie," she said. "Maybe you're not sure what I got to tell you, you may not want to hear it bad as you think. Most likely what you heard ain't really what happened."

"I want the truth, Mrs. Annie, whatever it might be."

She stared up at the cross again before she began. "Well sir, when the Yankees first came into Oakman they burned down pretty much everything, 'cept for the churches and a few houses. They didn't burned nothin' that belonged to Daniel Brewer 'cause they believed he was on their side, same as what you been told. No doubt, first Yankee solders what came along the railroad tracks stopped to water their horses, one of Daniel Brewer's slaves axed him where they was from. They told'em Pennsylvania, and that's when they first begin to call them houses by that name. Called 'em Pennsylvania Freedom. Don't know when they quit callin' it Freedom, and just called it Pennsylvania. That was even before my time. Well sir, you heard that Daniel Brewer didn't approve of slavery, didn't you?" She paused, took a deep breath and waited for me to answer.

"Yes ma'am, that's what I was told."

"Well sir, it ain't so. That Daniel Brewer was good to his slaves 'cause he didn't want them tellin' what they knew, that he had several chillen down in them quarters. That what he didn't want told. Some of 'em he had, colored women wanted his children, some didn't. He wasn't so good as he was smart. He knew somethin' nobody else knew, he knew the South was gonna lose. He didn't want them slaves tellin' what they knew to no one, North or South. Too many of them to kill so he figured he better do somethin' so they wouldn't tell. He set it up so marshals came by an seen about them after the war and he convinced them that if they told, the marshal wouldn't come by no more. I always heared one of the colored women that already had two or three of his chillen was the one who killed him, cause she wasn't wantin' no more of 'em. He had some of them women that wanted to have him and some that didn't want him, too."

Mrs. Annie wiped her eyes and her brow again before she continued, getting off the subject a moment first.

"How do you know Froney? She didn't say nothin' but I saw the look on her face when she opened the doors. I know she know you."

I responded, "I met her at Mrs. Davis' house. Mrs. Davis was the first one to tell me about Daniel Brewer."

She continued, "Mrs. Laura, she didn't know the truth about Daniel Brewer. Never told her. She had enough grief without knowing that, too." I wanted to ask her to explain but felt she would without asking. "Daniel Brewer, he done left them slaves this land here on the river, you heared that, too, didn't you?" She paused again, waiting for me to answer. She continued. "What everybody roun' here forget is, 'cept for this here church and that there Lazarus Cemetery all this under water most of the year up until the forties and fifties. Up until they built them dams along the river, this was nothin' but one big mud hole up and down the river. Have to start a house four or five feet off the ground to keep it out of the water. Couldn't even think about buildin' one when it was raining. What that man left them slaves wasn't good for nothin' up until the government build them dams, and he knew that. That's why he left this here land. Course nobody lived here on the river after the war. All them free slaves come to Pennsylvania to live 'cause it was the only place down here that belonged to Colored people. That's why they came here. Didn't have much but them houses and the land they was sittin' on, but they had that and that kept 'em out of the rain and gave them a place to build a fire to stay warm. I was born down there in Pennsylvania in 1880. Before that I don't know for sure what's true, but I 'spect that other about Daniel Brewer true, too. Miz Ruthie married that old Harlan Smart. My Mama, she worked for the Gibbons. She always say Miz Ruthie's parents done kept her too close, that why she took up with Harlan Smartt. My mama say Miz

Ruthie didn't know enough about a man to know he wasn't no good. He came around with his father shoein' horses and sellin' whiskey out from under the seat of his wagon, what he didn't drink on the way over here from Baldwin County. That Harlan Smartt started makin' eyes at Miz Ruthie and she didn't do nothin' but make eyes back. My mama said it wasn't no time til she was with a baby and they married and was living in the house with the Gibbons. She lost that baby 'cause he had her down one night and kicked her in the stomach sayin' he don't want no baby. My mama always say Miz Ruthie didn't know enough to kill him right then and there so she wouldn't have to live her life with him. Anyway, I used to go with my mama to the Gibbons' house and help her take care of Miz Carrie Gibbon's kitchen, that was Miz Ruthie's mama. Miz Ruthie had Miz Mollie Jean and later the Gibbons build them that house what Miz Laura was born into and came back to when she got old."

While Mrs. Watkins stopped to rest and cry a little, I tried to take it all in. Why I had not deciphered the initials on the back of the brooch before now I wasn't sure. I guess since I became involved with looking for someone named Smartt, I put it out of my mind. This was Ruth Lorena's Gibbons Smartt's cameo brooch, Mollie Jean and Laura's Belle's mother, Harlan Smart's wife, the brooch had been given to her before she married. Of course, I still did not know how it ended up in the fireplace, but I was sure Annie was going to tell me if I gave her enough time.

She continued. "When the Gibbons build them that new house, that's when I went to work for them. I was just a girl myself. Miz Ruthie had a terrible time. That Harlan Smartt he cussed and slapped her all the time. Drank all the time just like his sorry daddy. Miz Ruthie, she was always making excuses, saying he can't help the way he is. So anyway, I tried to do all I could for her and Miz Mollie. Then Miz Ruthie she came along pregnant again and she say things would be better, but nothin' goin' to make this man better. He done kicked the life out of one baby already. Well, sir, just about the time she goin' have that baby she fell down them stairs in that house. I always say that Harlan Smartt done got drunk and pushed her down them stairs, but Miz Ruthie left this world sayin' he didn't."

Annie had to compose herself before she continued at all. She wiped her eyes several times and glanced back and forth at the cross before she went on.

"I went to work that morning and old Mr. Harlan told me Miz Ruthie done fallen down them stairs and he put her in the bedroom downstairs. He told me to go take care of my 'missy'. I went in that bedroom and never seen anybody so pale in all my life, before or since. I pulled them covers back it looked to me she done lost all the blood she had. I hollered and axed that man what he done to my Miz Ruthie and she pulled me down to her as best she could, weak as she was, and told me she fell down the stairs, but I tell her quit lying for this man that he ain't no good. I hollered again and axed him if he sent for the doctor and he just sat there in that chair, drinking like he always do. Didn't answer me at all. I told Miz Ruthie I was goin' to get the doctor and Miz Carrie and I'd be right back, and for her to hold on. I was scared to leave her with that man, but there wasn't much else I could do. She pulled me down close to her again and told me to take care of Miz Mollie and this chile that's coming now, and I told her she goin' take care of them, but I's got to hurry and get the doctor. So, I ran across town to old Doctor John's office and told him Miz Ruthie's done fell down the stairs and her baby was coming, and she was bleeding real bad, that it looked like she done lost all the blood she had, and for him to hurry. He told me to ride with him back to the house, but I had to go fetch Miz Carrie."

She took several deep breaths and wiped her eyes before continuing the story.

"I ran fast as I could to the Gibbons' house and while Miz Carrie got dressed, I hooked up her buggy, hollering for her to hurry, that Miz Ruthie hurt real bad and her baby coming. Miz Carrie came and got in the buggy and I drove that horse back over to Miz Ruthie's house fast it would go."

Annie wiped her tears again and slowed her tone before she went on. I tried to imagine her rapid trip back and forth across town as she talked.

"We were too late. Miz Ruthie was dead. The doctor had took that little baby girl from her before it died, but he couldn't save Miz Ruthie. She had lost too much of her blood. Miz Carrie she fell across that bed where Miz Ruthie as laying and cried loud, so loud, I know Miz Ruthie heard it in heaven. It made my blood run cold. The doctor he handed me that little baby girl to clean up and axed me if I ever hear Miz Ruthie say what she goin' to name it if it was a girl. I told him she was goin' to name it Miss Laura Belle. I took that baby out to the kitchen to give it a bath and passed that devil Harlan Smartt sittin' there drinkin'. He never once axed me nothin'. He never axe me once if Miz Ruthie was dead or alive, or if was a girl or boy I was holdin'. Didn't axe me nothin'! I told that little girl I would take care of her and her sister as long as it took for them to get away from this sorry daddy of theirs. Wasn't none of their fault that he was the devil. As soon as Miz Carrie leaves Miz Ruthie's bedside, I begged her not to let Harlan Smartt put me out of that house. I told her I done promised Miz Ruthie I'd watch after Miz Mollie and Miz Laura and I wanted her to see that he not put me out. I couldn't see everything, I tried, but I couldn't stop everything."

Mrs. Annie broke down and cried into her handkerchief. This time her crying was also uncontrollable. I put my arm around her shoulder without saying a world. I wasn't sure if I had done the right thing until she turned her head toward my chest and cried even harder. She composed herself after a time. As she removed her head from my chest, she took her handkerchief and attempted to pat my shirt dry. I assured her it was all right and offered her the handkerchief from my pocket, believing her was too wet to be of any further use. She continued.

"Well sir, I went to raisin' those two girls as best I could. I wasn't seventeen myself when Miz Laura come into this world. When she was first born we spent most of the time over to the Gibbons' house, but pretty soon that Harlan Smartt say we can't stay over there no more, that he want his'n girls at home where they belongs. He cuss them girls and slap them just like he done Miz Ruthie, but I stood between 'em all I could. Then when Miz Laura about three or four years old, Miz Ruthie's father come to tell him he going to have him made Sheriff of Oakman. Mr. Riley, that was Miz Ruthie's father, he told that old Harlan Smartt it was high time be became somethin' for those two girls of his because he never was nothin' for Miz Ruthie. Mr. Riley told Harlan Smartt he goin' to have him made the Sheriff of Oakman and he better do right or he'd see them girls be taken away from him. Now he didn't care nothin' about them girls, but he did care bout that money and he know that if they go, the money go with 'em. So, they made him sheriff in 1900 or 1901, I ain't for sure. I thought for a time that he was changin', but he was only changin' so Mr. Riley and Miz Carrie could see him. That all was just a show of changin' so they could see. Miss Mollie was about thirteen or fourteen when I began to see her change so much. She wouldn't come out of her room and she cried all the time. When I axed her what was wrong, she tell me nothin', tell me just leave her alone. I didn't know what to think was goin' on with that chile'. I talked to Miz Carrie and I told her that man was up to not good, but all she could see what Harlan Smartt wanted her to see. Then Mr. Riley, he died before the Christmas of 1904. Then there wasn't nobody to do nothin' with that Harlan Smartt. He started drinkin' again, just like before, and he told me he don't want me liven' in his house no more. He told me to move back down to Pennsylvania where I belong. He say Miss Mollie plenty old enough to raise Miz Laura now. Them two girls cried and begged him not to send me away, but he told me if I don't leave, he'd arrest me for stealin' and put me in jail. Mr. Riley, he dead, Miz Carrie, she don't see nothin' and this Harlan Smart, he's 'The Law.' I had no choice, I couldn't do them girls no good in jail. So, I left. I broke my promise to Miz Ruthie, but there wasn't nothin' else I could do."

Again, Mrs. Watkins broke down and cried uncontrollably, but she continued through her tears.

"I wanted to stay with them girls but there was nothin' I could do. So, I left, but every chance I got, I slipped off up there so I could see them. When I see Sheriff Smartt around town, I run up to his house and see them and tell them if they ever needs me to come to

Pennsylvania and axe for me and people down there would show them where I stay. Pretty soon, I stopped seein' them at all. When I'd go to the house, they wouldn't open the door and I never seen them around town or nothin'. Miz Mollie, she stopped goin' to school altogether, so I couldn't even see her walkin' at a distance. I went and see Miz Carrie to tell her that Harlan Smartt is bad to those chillen, but she 'bout lost all her mind when Mr. Riley died, and she don't listen to me at all. She say I just upset 'cause he put me out of the house. But it ain't so, I know somethin bad's goin' on. Then about February of 1905, I hears this Sawyer boy he's arrested for beatin' and rapin' Miz Mollie. I slipped up to the house to see Miz Mollie. She come out on that porch and she begs me to help her get away from that father of hers. While she cryin', that Harlan Smartt slip up behind me and say he done warned me once that if he ever see me around there again he'd arrest me. He took out his pistol and shot at me, tell me I'm probably the one that sent that nigger over here to his daughter. I ran all the way home and I didn't know what to do. I just cried for months and didn't know what to do. I thought I might go and kill that Harlan Smartt, but I was scared he would kill me and still have my girls. I just didn't know what to do."

Mrs. Watkins was beginning to stand, and I helped her in an upright position. She placed her cane on the floor and started out of the church. There was a look of determination and anger on her face as she said, "Help me out here to this Lazarus Cemetery and I'll tell you all there is to tell about that devil Harlan Smartt!"

Her pace was faster than before, but still, very slow. I wasn't sure she could walk that far, but I was also quite certain there would be no stopping her.

Mrs. Watkins told me to, "Get them foldin' chairs up in the front of the church so we can sit out here."

By the time she directed me to get the chairs, she had moved out the doors and down the steps toward the cemetery with her cane hitting the ground faster than ever before. She had come upon the gate of Lazarus Cemetery before I joined her and was attempting to get it open. I leaned the chairs against my car and moved the gate back on its one rusty hinge, so she could enter. She did so and waited for me to return with the chairs before she moved again. She directed me to open the two chairs directly in front of the Lazarus Tree. Then she sat down, very out of breath. I put a hand on her twisted back and asked her if she was all right. In between gasps for air she said she would be as soon as she caught her breath.

She finally did get her wind back. She took several deep breaths while looking up at the Lazarus Tree before she continued her story. The anger that had been in her face on her way to the cemetery was replaced again by sorrow as we sat inside the cemetery fence and she continued her story.

"There's a lot of pain and sufferin' here in this ground, but no more than right there under that tree." She used her cane to point at the Lazarus Tree. There was terrible pain in her face, but no tears. She had cried all she could in the church. "I didn't see Miz Mollie no more for a long time. I worried myself thin trying to figure out what I could do 'bout her and Miz Laura and that man they havin' to live with. I thought I might just take them and run away, but runnin' cost money and I didn't have none. Well sir, six or seven months went by, and I was sittin' out on my porch down there in Pennsylvania watchin' the white folks' fireworks goin up in the air and light' up the sky. Just like always, I was wonderin' what I could do for my girls. All of a sudden, Miz Mollie come runnin' up on the porch tellin' me I gots to run, that I gots to get everybody to run. That the first time I ever knowed Miss Mollie is with a baby. She's a-holdin' her stomach and tellin' me everybody gots to run and get out of Pennsylvania. Then she grabs her stomach real hard and she hollers out loud and falls to her knees right out there on my porch. So, I grabs her up and takes her and puts her on my bed, and I feel that baby comin'. I tell her I never dreamed that Nathan Sawyer really had her, told her I thought it was a lie. She still screamin' that I got to get everybody out, that they be coming. I ain't listening to her 'cause I got to get ready for this baby what's comin'."

Mrs. Annie paused and looked at the Lazarus Tree before she went on. She pounded her cane against the ground and cussed

Harlan Smartt, then began again.

"That baby, it come on pretty quick and when it got here, I know what went on before I axed Miz Mollie. She was just like Miz Ruthie, she lost too much blood. It was too soon, too, this baby was way too early. It didn't have no hair or nails on its fingers. It was havin' a hard time gettin' air."

Mrs. Watkins had found some more tears and she cried them, then wiped her cheeks before she could go on.

"I told Miz Mollie, this ain't none of Nathan Sawyer's baby, this baby ain't got no Colored blood at all. I knowed before she answer me what went on. She says to me this her father's baby. Says she never know no other man, not ever. She told me her father find out she goin' to have a child, he fix it up where when that Nathan Sawyer come to the house he's waitin' behind the door upstairs and he hit him over the head when he comes to help her. Then that Harlan Smartt tells everybody Nathan raped her so when she begins to show with that baby he can say its' Nathan Sawyer's, that nigger that raped her. Then Miz Mollie, she tells me that Harlan Smartt told her if she don't sign a paper saying that Nathan Sawyer raped her, then he'll have him hung. Miz Mollie says she figure he better off alive in prison than dead on the end of a rope, so she signed the paper knowin' it ain't true."

She pounded the ground again with her cane and cried for Miss Mollie Jean and continued.

"Then at all once while she holdin' that little baby in her arms she starts tellin' me again that I got to get everybody out of Pennsylvania 'cause they is comin' to burn us out, and I calmed her down and axed her what in the world she talkin' 'bout. She say two men she don't know come to see Harlan Smartt that night and tell him they need that land down there for the city. They say Miz Ruthie was some kinda kin to Daniel Brewer and her family got land right next to it, cross the railroad tracks. They tell Harlan Smartt that if there ain't nothing or nobody on that land, then he can claim it as Miz Ruthie's since she dead. Next thing she know, two more mens comes to the house. She knew them, but she didn't know their names. Harlan Smartt tells them to go down and tell everybody down there at the white folks' July 4th celebration that there is typhoid in Pennsylvania and set them shacks on fire and don't let no niggers out, and if they try to run, shoot them dead."

Again, she had to pause and compose herself. If it were possible, she looked older than she had before.

"I guess that's what they did, cause it wasn't no time before I hear hollerin' and shootin' out there. Miz Mollie, she grabbed me and pulled me down to her like her mama had done and tells me to take her mama's brooch and gloves out of her purse and hide them so her baby could have them to remember. She says that the only things she get out of the house without that daddy of hers seein' her. I took and put them up in that old chimney to hide them like Miz Mollie wanted me to. I knew all about that chimney, that had been in my aunties' house. I used to play in it when I was little. One time I tried to climb up that old chimney. Then I went back and got that little baby girl breathin' so slow and hard and brought it and put it down in a chair so I could go help Miz Mollie out that bed. That hollerin' is so loud now I can hardly stand it. Miz Mollie, she's cryin' and tryin' to get out of bed, but she so weak from havin' that baby too soon that she can't get up. I turned to go back in the bedroom and all at once a torch come through the window and the bed and the room and Miz Mollie was on fire."

Miss Annie bowed her head without a sound for several minutes. No crying, no noise at all. Then she raised her head and began again in a slow methodical tone.

"I tried to go back in there and get her out, but I couldn't. The fire was just too hot. Miz Mollie, she quit cryin' real quick. Last I saw her she was fallin' back on the bed with that pretty red hair of hers all burned up. Red, just like Miz Ruthie's. I grabbed up that baby and ran out the door to the woods behind my house. It was dark back there even with the fires burning, nobody ever see one Black woman runnin' into the woods. I sat out there all night rockin' that baby and watchin' them houses burn. People hollerin' and runnin' all night. The white men, they pushin' back and making' 'em stand between the houses while they burn. The white mens, they keep hollering' we can't let the typhoid spread. If anybody try to run, they shoot'em. Some of 'em couldn't tolerate the heat from the flames and they ran. They all buried down there in one grave."

She took her cane and pointed to the nine graves at the northwest corner of the cemetery that I knew to be marked 'July 5, 1905.' Her tone was slower and more sorrowful than before as she continued.

"Me, I rocked that baby all night. Hugged and sang to it and promised it Harlan Smartt wouldn't ever know it was in this world. Only thing I could think of was this: Miz Mollie didn't tell me what the name that baby girl. I told that baby we'd wait 'til morning and see what she look like 'fore we name her and I just kept rockin' and singin' out there in them woods. 'Fore the sun came up all them white men left out, so nobody know just who was who. First light I could see there wasn't nothing left but stone, ashes, and rubble. Some of it was still smokin', but no house left at all. I unwrapped Miz Mollie's baby to see what its face looked like in the sun, see what kind of name it needed."

She paused and wiped her tears again, taking a deep breath before she went on.

"I guess I really knew that baby done died a long time ago. It just came to soon. Too young to breathe out here in this world, needed to stay in its mama longer so it could breathe right. I named that baby anyway, 'cause everybody need a name. I named that baby Miz Ruthie 'cause I knowed Miz Mollie would like that. I waited for the sun to go down again and when it did, I went and took Miz Mollie out of them ashes and pulled her back there into the woods with her baby. Then I walked over to Miz Carrie's in the dark and took the rug off her front porch and the horse and carriage out of her barn and drove over there to them woods where Miz Mollie and Miz Ruthie was, rolled them up in that rug, put them across Miz Carrie's wagon and brought them to this here Lazarus Cemetery. Took me might near all night to dig that grave through them roots around that tree, but it didn't matter. I'd dug that grave for a year if it would keep my Miz Mollie and her baby away from that Harlan Smartt. Near mornin', I put them in that grave and asked that Lazarus Tree and the Lord to look over them, not let that Harlan Smartt ever find them. I buried them up there close to that tree 'cause I didn't know if Miz Mollie mind if her and her baby be buried with Colored people, so I put her up there where nobody ever been buried, Black or White. Years later I married Mr. George Watkins, as good a man as he could be. I axed him to make me a marker say 'Mother and Child' and put it up there on Miz Mollie and Miz Ruthie's grave. I told him not to axe me no questions, just do what I axe. He left this earth never axin' once who was buried there. Long time ago, he built me a bench around that Lazarus Tree. Come all the way around on either side right up to the marker so's I can come here and sit and talk to my girls. 'Course, that bench been gone a long time now."

She had used all her tears again and by now she had to be very tired.

She continued, and told me concerning the horses, "I just turned 'em loose and let 'em go. I knew they'd find their way back home. Next day I hear the white folks saying' some Colored boys stole some fireworks and started the fire what burned up Pennsylvania."

Mrs. Watkins stood up from her chair and turned, looking from my car, to the Lazarus Tree. Then she paused and made it a point to look at me directly in the eye speaking, "Mr. Wallace, take me for a ride in your automobile, and I'll tell you the rest of this story. I'll show where what I haven't told you be."

I had to think for a minute. I certainly had no objection to taking her anywhere she wanted to go, but I wasn't sure I wanted to hear anymore. I could not believe there was any more to tell. Mrs. Watkins had made the decision for me. By the time I looked up she was by the car trying to open the door. I moved to the passenger door and opened it, telling Mrs. Watkins we would be on our way as soon as I returned the chairs to the church.

She directed me onto the interstate to the west, instructing me to take the Ferry Street exit. Once we descended the off-ramp, we went out through a very old section of Oakman that was full of dilapidated houses, some being repaired, other that appeared as though a wind would finish blowing them to the ground. Shortly we came across the Lee Street entrance to the Oakman Cemetery. Mrs. Watkins directed me with the accuracy of a ship navigator through cobblestone streets that crisscrossed the cemetery.

We eventually ended up in the old part of the cemetery where she directed me to stop and park. There I helped her out of the car, and we moved slowly though the multitude of headstones that were as old as the ones under the Lazarus Tree, but not nearly as much in need of repair. We stopped at an old iron fence that held perhaps fifteen or twenty graves within its circumference. I had not finished counting the markers before Mrs. Watkins spoke again.

She pointed over the fence at a group of graves toward the back of this plot and stated, "that's Mr. Riley and Miz Carrie's graves there. Then Miz Ruthie's is off there to the side next to that little grave. That's the baby Harlan Smartt kicked outta her. This is where Miss Mollie ought to be, here with her family. It's all right for Miz Laura to be buried down in Cornerville, she got her husband to be beside. Miz Mollie and her baby need to be here with her family."

Two things struck me as strange as we stood and looked across the fence. I wondered, as she steadied herself on my arm, how she knew where Mrs. Davis had been buried. I had said nothing to her about Mr. Phillips' inquiry. Then I strained my eyes looking for Harlan Smartts' grave in the vicinity of Ruthie's.

"Mrs. Watkins," I asked, "how did you know where Mrs. Davis was buried?"

She stared at me for a moment as if she wondered why I didn't know she was the one who had sent Lawyer Phillips the anonymous letter and responded stating, "Miz Laura gave me them letters to that funeral home and that lawyer years ago. Knew if she died before me, I see they got instructions on what to do. Had my picture in the paper when I turned ninety-five years old. That the first time Miz Laura know I was still alive. Had my picture in the paper when I turned one hundred, too. Guess they figure they better get one when I turned ninety-five 'cause they might not get one when I was a hundred.

Didn't have one on my hundred and fifth birthday, guess they's waitin' to see if I make a hundred and ten."

Her tone was very matter of fact, as if there was no question in her mind that she would see her one hundred and tenth birthday.

I strained my eyes toward the headstones again, looking for Harlan Smartt's grave before I asked my second question. "Where's Harlan Smartt's grave, Mrs. Watkins?"

She laughed that low, graveled laugh again before she answered. "Miz Carrie done lost her mind completely by the time that Harlan Smartt got his neck broke. She got enough of it back, though, to say she wasn't havin' that devil buried nowhere near her baby girl that he caused so much pain. Told 'em to take him and throw his body in the river for all she cared, but he wasn't gonna be buried next to her baby. Guess they took him and buried him with some of that trash of his over in Baldwin County. May have weighted him down like Miz Ruthie said and throwed him off in the river. I never heard nobody say what became of his body. I knows what become of his soul. This is where Miz Mollie and her baby ought to be, with her folks."

She had turned and headed back toward the car before I knew she was moving and was again directing me toward our destination.

"Take me over to Miz Ruthie's and Miz Laura's house and I'll tell you all the rest."

What more could there possibly be? Surely by now I thought Mrs. Annie Watkins had told me everything, but obviously there was at least one more story to tell.

As we travelled back down the interstate, the river came into view. She pointed off to the left in sight of the river and showed me where Carrie's and Riley's house used to be.

She stated, "they tore it down years ago. Lord knows, it was about to fall in anyway. After Miz Carrie died, there just wasn't nobody to live in it anymore. They took Miz Laura to that chillen's home because Miz Carrie couldn't take care of herself, let alone a little girl. I woulda kept her with me, but they wouldn't let no Colored woman have no White girl back in those days."

I pulled up in front of what I now knew to be not only Mrs. Laura Davis' house, but also the house that the Gibbons had built for their daughter and her husband, Harlan Smartt. The house Mrs. Davis had been born into. The house her mother died in bringing Laura into the world. The same house in which her father had terrorized her and Mollie Jean, and eventually the house where, he, too, had met his end. I looked at the large wooden structure in a different light than I had the first time I saw it. I wondered as I moved around the car why in the world Mrs. Laura Davis had chosen to make what, for her, had been such an awful place her home a second time. When she was a child, she had no choice, but as an adult, I could not imagine returning to the memories it surely must have held. I moved around to help Mrs. Watkins out of the car and she immediately began to move up the walkway and around the back of the house. Her fatigue was beginning to show. She moved much more slowly now than she had from the church to the Lazarus Cemetery or from the car to the Gibbons' family plot.

"Come on here," she said, "there's a swing 'round back here we can sit in, and I'll tell you the rest of what I know, and I'll tell you what I want you to do for Miz Mollie and her baby."

There was, in fact, a long, wooden swing mounted under a large pecan tree in the rear of the house. We moved to it and had a seat. Mrs. Watkins commented once, as she was sitting down, before she took a moment to catch her breath again.

"Guess they tear this one down too, ain't no one to live in it, either." She sat staring at the balcony from which Miss Mollie had begged her for help, the place where Nathan Sawyer had entered the house and then ended up in prison, and the place where Harlan Smartt had met his well-deserved death. There was a look of hatred and then sorrow in her face as she sat, staring up the railing trying to catch her breath, and she looked, I felt, very much as she had looked at Miss Ruthie, Mollie's baby girl, the night they burned Pennsylvania to the ground. Her lips were white and her brow, wet with perspiration, as she sat undoubtedly seeing it all in her mind. Finally, Mrs. Watkins caught her breath. The pink color of her lips returned,

146

and she began to tell, as she said, all the rest of what she knew.

"Now I knows I got that Harlan Smartt where I needs for him to be. I came here to his house and told him Miss Mollie Jean had come to me and told me what he done done to her. I tells him I know now why he done kept her in this house all these months. I knew in my heart I couldn't help Miss Mollie no more, her suffering done over, but I could help Miz Laura. So, I tell him I helped Miz Mollie run away, that I gives her money to go to Nashville to have that baby. I tells him I know who will help a young girl in trouble like she was, and I tells him I'm comin' back over here to raise Miz Laura, keep the same thing from happen' to her what done happened to Miz Mollie. Then I tells him if he gives me any trouble, I'll have Miz Mollie come back and tell all the White folks what he done to her and he'll be down there at Poplar Bluff where he need to be instead of Nathan Sawyer."

She laughed a cold, deep laugh before she continued There was a genuine tone of hatred in her voice, of obvious contempt for Harlan Smartt. As well there should be. She was not glad Miss Mollie had to endure his sadistic treachery, but she was glad she had taken the opportunity to use it for Miss Laura's welfare.

She continued, "Lord, you shoulda seen the look on his face when I told him I see Miz Mollie and she done told me what kinda way she was in. That the first time I ever seen that devil scared of somethin'. He didn't argue with me at all. He thought I for sure knew what I was talkin' about, cause he ain't let nobody see that child since she be with that baby. He believed everything I said. That's when he told them reporters he put Miss Mollie on that train for Nashville to his sisters'. That when he let everybody see him lightin' out on horseback toward Nashville. He didn't go nowhere but over there to Baldwin County and lay around drunk with that trash of his for two or three days. I moved in over there while he was gone and started raising Miz Laura like she ought to be raised. She was about eight years old at that time. She had an idea of what went on with Miz Mollie. She told me her sister cried all the time. She even told me about her daddy slippin' round that house in the middle of the night.

I told her he ain't goin' to be slippin' 'round that house no more, not while I be there."

She continued, "Well sir, things went along there good for several years. That Harlan Smartt, I done thought I made him respectable. He was good to Miz Laura and he talks to me like I'm his mama. He don't give me or anybody no backtalk and if he's drinkin', I ain't been seein' it. Yes sir, we was doin' fine. All I wanted was to get Miz Laura grown, then she could get away from that man. I always thought I'd tell her 'bout Miz Mollie when she was old enough, I didn't never tell her. She done left this earth without knowin' what become of her sister. I was meanin' to tell her, but I just never got to it."

Mrs. Annie bowed her head like she had at Lazarus Cemetery, but as before, she didn't cry or make a sound. When she began to talk again, that slow, deliberate tone had returned to her voice. "That Harlan Smartt, he fooled me. If he hadn't broke his neck when he fell from that two-story porch, I'da broke it myself. See, I puts Miz Laura to bed one night when she was eleven years old, and goes down to the river to sit with my auntie. Them houses they built down there on the river after the White folks burned Pennsylvania ain't too good. They's cold in the winter and hot in the summer. Ain't got no well yet and they's takin' water out of the river to do what they need. Colored people ain't got much a nothin', 'cause what they did have burned up in that fire. What folks do have houses is sleepin' on the floor. I goes one night to sit with her. I didn't leave 'til late, after I puts Miz Laura to bed. I didn't even tell that Harlan Smartt that I was goin'. So, he think I'm in my room there at the kitchen. Come back 'fore sunup the next mornin' and went up to check on my Miz Laura, and I finds her all doubled up, in the corner of that room, crying. Her little gown be torn, and her lip is bleedin' and she crying so low. I screamed to the Lord that I kill that man for sure this time. He done fooled me. Now he done the same thing to Miz Laura that he done to Miz Mollie. Miz Laura, she hold me so tight and cries, and my heart hurts so bad. I shouldn't a left this child, I shoulda taken this child to the river with me. Lord knows I shouldn't a left her in this house with that man. I was tryin' to hold Miz Laura and I was axin' her if her daddy done hurt her bad, and she pointin' out there on that porch, tellin' me her daddy is out there. She tell me she pushed him away and he's out there on that porch. I left Miz Laura and got the poker from that fireplace up in that room and I went out on that porch and told that man I goin' to kill him for sure this time. Shoulda killed him for what he did to Miz Mollie.

"Told him I gonna beat him to death this time. When I walked out on that porch, the sun was just comin' up. I looked around for him out there and finally found him layin' there in the yard." She took her cane and pointed at the ground just below the balcony. No tears this time, she was glad Harlan Smartt was dead. She was seeing his twisted body lying there on the ground again, and I thought for a moment she might smile, but she didn't.

"Ain't no more than he deserved. Shame Miz Laura had to be the one, but it wasn't no more than he deserved."

Mrs. Annie stopped and stared up at the balcony while I went back over what happened in my mind. Apparently, Harlan Smartt had discovered she was not in her kitchen room and decided to take the opportunity to return to his old habits. Although she hadn't said, I believed this was the first time Annie had left Laura alone since moving back in. Harlan Smartt had, no doubt, been waiting for this occasion the whole time without Annie's knowledge. He had come to what had been Mollie's room to terrorize Laura like he had her sister. Laura had seized some moment, one second perhaps, when he was off-guard and had pushed him just enough for him to lose his balance and fall over the rail. Fate or luck, I do not know which, would have him break his neck. If he had been pushed to the ground and not died, he would have surely been furious and returned to her room.

Mrs. Annie continued, "Deputy Stanley, he come by to get Sheriff Smartt, while I was up there trying to comfort my Miz Laura, tellin' her she didn't mean to do it. She didn't understand what he was goin' to do to her. She just thought she had pushed her daddy over the rail. She was cryin' and sorry she did it. She was too young

149

for me to 'splain she ought to be glad. It was too late for me to do anything with Harlan Smartt's body, the sun was full up and Deputy Stanley was knockin' at the door. So, I went down and let him in. I always knowed he was a better man than Harlan Smartt anyway. I brought him upstairs and told him what done happened. Told him that's why Miz Mollie runned away, 'cause this man was doin' the same thing to her. He looked all 'round that room and out on that balcony, and he tells me to get Miz Laura dressed and take her over to my auntie's where I been all night. He tells me to go 'round back of town along the river, and not let no one see us. If anybody axed, he says to tell them me and Miz Laura been over there all night. He tells me to leave a note down there by the door to tell Harlan Smartt that where we be if he be lookin' for us. He tells me to tell my auntie to say the same thing, that we been there all night. Deputy Stanley say he be by to get us later and whoever with him for me to be actin' like I don't know nothin' 'bout Harlan Smartt bein' dead. Nothin' at all. He came by my auntie's just like he say he would, had two other deputies with him. He say it look like Sheriff Smartt goin' to maybe sleep out there on that balcony where it's cool. Says he been drinkin' cause they done found a bottle out there on that porch. Musta lost his balance and fell. Tells me like I don't know that Harlan Smartt he done broke his neck and died in that fall. See, I knowed that Deputy Stanley was a better man than most. He shoulda been sheriff 'stead of that Harlan Smartt."

She paused before continuing and appeared to be in deep thought. She was, I'm sure, seeing all the things in her mind that she had not seen in the last eighty-five years. All the death and destruction. The pain and the sorrow held in for a lifetime, more than a lifetime. Mrs. Annie Mae Watkins had carried a burden of guilt for a lifetime that she was not responsible for. It was Harlan Smartt who was to blame for the suffering of the people she loved. He died not knowing any feelings of love of remorse. Annie had carried it for him. Just as the Lazarus Tree had tried to reach out to protect the people who rested under its limbs, she had tried to protect 'her girls.'

"I guess that's 'bout all I knows to tell," said Mrs. Annie. "Wasn't long, they came and got Miz Laura. Say Miz Carrie all they is, and she can't take care of Miz Laura. I told'em I stay right in this house and raise Miz Laura., but the state people told me I can't. So, they took her away to the chillen's home. I wrote her, and she wrote me for a while. Then I got a letter from a woman there at the home tellin' me not to write Miz Laura no more, say it's better if she forget this life here. I wrote a time or two anyway, but the letters come back unopened. Miz Laura, she got grown and became a teacher down there at that school. Just like me gonna get that brooch and them gloves out of the fireplace, she gonna come back and see me. I never did get over there and get Miz Ruthie's things. Miz Laura didn't make it back here to Oakman 'til she was almost an old woman herself. Thought sure I was dead. Didn't know 'til my ninety-fifth birthday that I was still alive. She came to see me then, been seein' one another regular right up 'til she died. I might should a told her everything about Miz Mollie and her baby, but I just never did. She made a good life for herself, wasn't no need. Didn't marry 'til late, no chillen to visit her grave. Course, she had forty years of chillen there at that home; they'll come by, I 'spect."

She was deep in thought again, staring at the ground, looking for the words to continue. "Now sir, I done told you all you wanted to know, maybe more. I need you to do somethin' for me. I don't know how we gonna do it, but we gots to try. I wants you to help me get Miz Mollie and her baby moved over there with her folks. She and that baby need to be next to Miz Ruthie, with Mr. Riley and Miz Carrie. That's where they belonged all these long years. I want to see 'em there 'fore I die. You the only one, besides me, know this whole story and ain't nobody alive to hurt with it now. You gots to help me make it right."

"Ms. Annie," I finally spoke, "I'm not even sure where to begin. It's been such a long time. We would have to prove that Mollie and here baby are there in Lazarus Cemetery. I don't honestly know if it can be done."

"You will try, won't you?"

What else could I say but that I would do all that I could?

Mrs. Watkins directed me back across town to her house where Froney and her daughter were waiting. She told me along the way that Froney was her husband's granddaughter by his and his first wife's son. She had come to Oakman many years ago, pregnant and unmarried, looking for her grandfather who she knew would help her. Froney was unaware that he had passed away. Annie had taken Froney in and helped her raise this child as if they were her own.

Their devotion to her was obvious as they met us at the curb to help her inside when we arrived.

Somewhere in her mind I was certain Annie had tried to make up for Mollie and Laura through Froney and her daughter. Although Annie was not to blame for their fate, I hoped in my heart that Froney and her daughter had helped ease her pain.

I spent the rest of the evening recanting the entire story to Mary. She cried, as did I, for Mollie, her baby, and Laura.

19

ON MONDAY MORNING I DROVE TO CORNERVILLE and without an appointment, went to see Mr. Phillips, not knowing what else to do. I told him Annie's whole incredible story and assured him I was as anxious to have Mollie and her baby moved to the city cemetery as she was. It was not a question of whether Mollie and her baby would rest better, it was Annie Mae Watkins that needed to rest from the burden she had carried most of her life.

Mr. Phillips was honest in telling me that he really had no idea himself just exactly how to proceed. He did assure me, just as I had assured Annie, that he would try. Over the next several months Reverend Young and Thomas Whatley, attorney-at-law, formed an organization known as the Children of Pennsylvania. The organization took on several projects with its volunteer membership. One of its main objectives was genealogical research into the background of present-day Black citizens of Oakman. They were in hopes that if one or more descendants of Daniel Brewer could be verified, they could hold the city responsible for the land taken away from them in 1905.

To date, only one document has been found to substantiate the city's claim of ownership. The only documentation found to show legal ownership by Ruth Gibbons Smartt was the entry in the city probate book which Tommy and I found. Ruth Gibbons Smartt did inherit land adjacent to their twenty-three acres. There has, to date, been no deed found to prove any ownership of Pennsylvania by her or any other White descendants of Daniel Brewer. The land, according to his will, would revert to the city of Oakman if not occupied for a period of ten years. Whether or not Harlan Smartt acted alone, or with the blessing of city officials at the time, remains to be seen. Since he died only three years after the destruction of Pennsylvania, it should be evident to anybody that he had nothing to do with the city's relentless march across Pennsylvania Road. From all indications, the city of Oakman began cutting the Black population off from Pennsylvania within weeks after it burned. The road that had gone from there directly to Lazarus Cemetery had been completely obliterated within five years after the fire. Whoever was responsible, undoubtedly believed they had to cut off the original inhabitants of Pennsylvania from their home forever.

Over the next several months, Mrs. Annie Mae Watkins and I were interviewed by Judge Paul Saddix. In October of 1988, he ordered the grave marked 'Mother and Child' at Lazarus Cemetery exhumed. He further ordered that an autopsy be performed on the remains found in that grave, and if the facts revealed by that autopsy bore out the statements made by Mrs. Watkins, the remains were to be re-interred in the Oakman Cemetery, the part of the cemetery known as the Gibbons Family Plot.

The state forensic pathologist, Dr. Malcolm Anderson, who performed the autopsy on the skeletal remains found in that grave concluded that they were the remains of a Caucasian female approximately fifteen to twenty years of age and a female fetus of approximately twenty-eight week's gestation. He also found that the woman had had red hair and had been exposed to extreme heat prior to or after her death. No identification was possible due to advanced decomposition and lack of comparative medical evidence. Judge Saddix ordered that these remains be re-interred in the city cemetery as he promised, based on these findings.

On October 21, 1988, Mary, Reverend Young, Thomas Hadley, Annie Mae Watkins, her daughter Mollie, Tommy, and I attended a graveside service for the burial of Miss Mollie Jean Smartt and her infant daughter Ruthie. As Reverend Young conducted the service, Mrs. Watkins moved to my side and asked if the funeral home director had put 'Miz Ruthie's brooch and gloves' in the casket as she had requested. I assured her he had.

In December of this same year, through the efforts of the

Children of Pennsylvania, Reverend Nathan Young, and Thomas Hadley, a pardon was granted to Nathan Sawyer by the governor. Unfortunately, the pardon was granted some three weeks after Mr. Sawyer's death.

Three days before the one-year anniversary of Mollie Jean's and Ruthie's burial in the Oakman City Cemetery, Froney Watkins called me at home. She said that Ms. Annie had requested that I go with them to the cemetery on Saturday, October 21, to place flowers on their graves. Upon arriving at Ms. Annie's house to accompany her to the cemetery, I was informed by Froney that Annie had passed away during the night at the age of one hundred nine. She had requested before her death that I go to the cemetery and place flowers on Mollie's and Ruthie's grave for her.

As I knelt down, placing Mrs. Annie's hand-picked arrangement on their graves. I discovered among the flowers a note addressed to me. It was written in the same unsteady style as was the card that Mrs. Annie had used to answer my ad about the brooch. I stood there in the Gibbons' family plot and I wept as I read it:

Dear Mr. Robert
"I hope with my passing there will be more men like you who do not care about the color of a person's skin. Men like you, who care because they know that we are all the same in the eyes of God. I thank you from my heart for helping. Do not cry for me, I can rest now as do Miss Mollie and her baby girl. My sleep with the Lord is welcome".

In the Spring, I visited Lazarus Cemetery for the last time. The city of Oakman had erected a historical marker at the gate to the cemetery giving a brief history. The Children of Pennsylvania had installed a bronze plaque at the foot of the Lazarus Tree where Mollie and her baby rested over eighty years. The plaque inscription commemorated a wooden sign that at one time had been attached to this stately tree.

"I am the resurrection and the life; he that believeth in me, though he were dead, yet shall he live. And whosoever liveth and believeth in me shall never die."

One other change had taken place since I first saw the Lazarus Tree. At the very far points of its massive reach, leaves were swaying in the wind coming across the river. There were only a few, but they were green and very much alive.